THE WORLD'S WORST TEACHERS

BOOKS BY DAVID WALLIAMS:

The Boy in the Dress
Mr Stink
Billionaire Boy
Gangsta Granny
Ratburger
Demon Dentist
Awful Auntie
Grandpa's Great Escape
The Midnight Gang
Bad Dad
The Ice Monster
FING

The World's Worst Children
The World's Worst Children 2
The World's Worst Children 3

ALSO AVAILABLE IN PICTURE BOOK:

The Slightly Annoying Elephant
The First Hippo on the Moon
The Bear Who Went Boo!
The Queen's Orang-utan
There's a Snake in My School!
Boogie Bear
Geronimo

David Walliams

THE WORLD'S WORST TEACHERS

Illustrated in glorious colour by **Tony Ross**

HarperCollins *Children's Books*

DAVID WALLIAMS

HEAD BOY

TONY ROSS

HOUSE CAPTAIN

For the
best teachers
in the world,
especially three of mine:
Mr George Paxton,
Mr Patrick Carpmael,
Mr Jim Grant
D.W.

For all my
teachers,
with their endless patience
T.R.

First published in Great Britain by HarperCollins *Children's Books* in 2019
HarperCollins *Children's Books* is a division of HarperCollins*Publishers* Ltd,
HarperCollins Publishers, 1 London Bridge Street, London SE1 9GF

The HarperCollins website address is www.harpercollins.co.uk

10 9 8 7 6 5 4 3 2 1

David Walliams and Tony Ross assert the moral right to be identified
as the author and illustrator of the work respectively. Printed and
bound in Germany by GGP Media GmbH, PöBneck.
Find out more about HarperCollins and the environment
at www.harpercollins.co.uk/green

From the desk of
David Walliams

Dear Reader,

There have been three volumes of the world's worst children: *The World's Worst Children*, then the imaginatively titled *The World's Worst Children 2*, which was inevitably followed by *The World's Worst Children 3*.

In those books, there were countless stories of GHASTLY children: the absolute worst of the worst, the crème de la phlegm. The nasty, the greedy, the grubby, the vain, the sneaky, the fussy, the lazy, the bossy, the boastful and, of course, most appallingly, the windy.

Now it is time for children everywhere to get their REVENGE, and wipe the smug grins off the faces of the grown-ups forever.

The tables have turned.

This is *The World's Worst Teachers*. Ten stories about teachers who make the world's worst children look like a church choir. They are the most LOATHSOME collection of grown-ups ever. These teachers are every child's worst nightmare.

So read on, if you dare.

David Walliams

SCHOOL REPORT

I would like to thank the following people for doing absolutely nothing:

Subject	Comments	Grade
Ann-Janine Murtagh *Executive Publisher*	*Ann-Janine finds that the work interferes with her talking.*	**F**
Tony Ross *My Illustrator*	*Doodles all day. Tony needs to buckle down and do some proper work.*	**F**
Paul Stevens *My Agent*	*Paul is depriving a village somewhere of a perfectly good idiot.*	**F-**
Charlie Redmayne *CEO*	UNDER SOME KIND OF DELUSION THAT HE IS IN CHARGE. CHARLIE NEEDS SERIOUS HELP.	**F**
Alice Blacker *My Editor*	*Alice set herself an extremely very low standard, which she has failed to reach.*	**F**
Kate Burns *Publishing Director*	KATE HAS REACHED ROCK BOTTOM AND HAS STARTED TO DIG.	**F**
Samantha Stewart *Managing Editor*	*The wheel may be turning, but the hamster is dead.*	**F**
Val Brathwaite *Creative Director*	*Eats textbooks.*	**F-**

SUBJECT	COMMENTS	GRADE
David McDougall *Art Director*	*Sleeps at his desk. Leaves puddles of drool on the floor.*	**F**
Sally Griffin *Designer*	*Sally is very interested in the environment. She spends all day staring out of the window.*	F
Matthew Kelly *Designer*	*Matthew has the attention span of a tadpole.*	**F-**
Elorine Grant *Deputy Art Director*	*It is a great pleasure when she is absent. Which is always.*	F
Kate Clarke *Designer*	*In a class of thirty, Kate came thirty-first.*	F
Tanya Hougham *My Audio Editor*	TANYA COULD GO FAR. THE FURTHER THE BETTER.	**F**
Geraldine Stroud *My PR Director*	*Full marks all round. What a dreadful swot.*	A+

David Walliams

Dear Sir/Madam,

I am writing in reply to your recent letter requesting me to write a foreword for **Mr David Walliams'** new publication, *The World's Worst Teachers*.

You are correct – I was Mr Walliams' headmistress for his time at **Curdle School for Deeply Unpleasant Children**. Walliams, as he was known then, was one of the most repulsive boys I have ever had the misfortune to teach. He was rude, loud and deeply irritating. So no change there, then. The boy showed no talent whatsoever for performing or writing. So, again, no change there, then.

Even as a child of ten, Mr Walliams was hefty, and would break any chair on which he sat. However, my abiding memory of him was his smell. In a word, rancid.

Wherever he waddled, the boy Walliams would leave a visible stink behind. A great cloud of green and yellow and brown that smelled worse than it looked – and it looked disgusting.

I am appalled, though not surprised, that Mr Walliams would dare to write a book called *The World's Worst Teachers*. Perhaps he should think about writing a book entitled *The World's WORST Pupil?* Because that is exactly what he was. That is, of course, if Mr Walliams even writes his own books, which, having perused his school reports again, I highly doubt.

His English teacher, Miss Vent, described him thus: "Walliams has the story-writing skills of a pebble. His spelling and grammar are atrocious, and his handwriting so poor I wondered if his story about a girl who goes to school dressed as a boy, or some such nonsense, was, in fact, in some kind of alien language."

Meanwhile, his History teacher, Mr Saga, called him: "Perhaps the stupidest child who has ever lived. Just yesterday he put his hand up and told me that there was only one World War, and that was World War Two."

For Science, Mr Conduct wrote: "His understanding of the workings of the human body is nil. Hardly surprising for a boy who talks only out of his bottom."

In French, Miss Cul-de-Sac commented: "The great oaf of a boy is only interested in knowing the French word for one thing, 'chocolate'. This is, as we all know, 'chocolat'."

As headmistress, I summed up his time at Curdle by writing on his final school report: "Walliams is the worst of the worst. Even though he failed every single exam, I never, ever, ever want to see him back at my school. If this buffoon does set foot on school premises again, there will be a riot. A riot by the teachers led by me, and we will tear down the school, brick by brick if we have to."

The mere thought of Mr Walliams is enough to make me want to spontaneously combust. So, in answer to your question about whether I would like to write the foreword for *The World's Worst Teachers*, I say this: I would rather eat my own foot. And I am a vegetarian.

Please never contact me again or I will call the police. Or, failing that, the army.

Yours furiously,

Miss Spleen

HEADMISTRESS OF CURDLE SCHOOL

CONTENTS

MR PENT'S
BALLS

ONCE UPON A TIMES TABLE, there was a Maths
teacher named Mr Pent. He certainly looked like a
textbook Maths teacher, with his wire-rimmed glasses,
brown suit and comb-over. However, Mr Pent was
anything *but* your average Maths teacher.

Oh no, he was one of the world's very worst teachers. That was because Mr Pent's every waking moment was taken up with one dark obsession.

Balls.

He had a deep loathing of them.

But where did this strange fixation with **spherical** objects come from?

Our story begins when Mr Pent was still a child. It is easy to forget that teachers were once children, but in most cases they were.

Some babies you knew immediately were destined to be teachers, because they were born with a teacherly scowl of disapproval on their face:

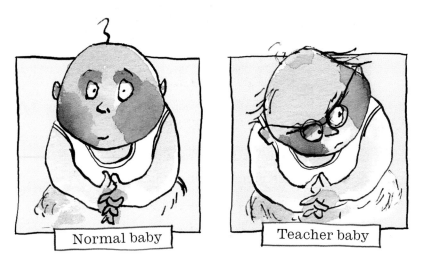

Normal baby   Teacher baby

As soon as he was put in his cot, Baby Pent was counting the beads above his head. Soon he was writing complex mathematical ᵉᑫᵘᵃᵗᶤᵒᶰˢ on the wall with his Alphabetti Spaghetti. It was when, as a toddler, he began giving his parents algebra homework that they knew for sure their little boy was destined to be a Maths teacher.

One day, when Master Pent was just ten* years old, he suffered a terrible accident.

The boy was struck on the head by a ball.

Not just any ball.

* That's 2 x 5, 7 + 3, 20 − 10, or 50 ÷ 5.

A DEMOLITION BALL.

As balls go, this has to be one of the biggest and **heaviest** there is. After all, it is made of steel and swung from a crane to destroy buildings.

BISH! BASH! BOSH!

Being a child whose fate it was to become a Maths teacher, it will not surprise you to learn that Master Pent had no time for toys or games or anything that might be considered fun. No, this mathematics-loving child filled his days with times tables, prime numbers, fractions, quadratic equations, trigonometry and (for most of us normal folk, the absolutely dreaded) long division.*

One rainy afternoon, Master Pent was on his way home from his school Maths Club. Maths Club was the world's most boring after-school club. Master Pent was, in fact,

---

* In some countries, long division is actually a form of torture. "NO! NO! NOT LONG DIVISION! ANYTHING BUT LONG DIVISION! I CONFESS!"

the **only** member. Other strong contenders for the world's most boring after-school club are:

Punctuation Club "

Standing-in-a-puddle Society

Basket-weaving for Beginners

TRAINSPOTTERS ANONYMOUS

Sitting-in-the-dark Society

STARING-AT-A-BLANK-WALL CLUB

Traffic-cone Appreciation Society

LATIN! LATIN! LATIN!

In Maths Club, Master Pent had just been learning all about pi, also known as π or 3.14. Pi is even more boring than it sounds, and it sounds cataclysmically boring. It is a mathematical constant, the ratio of a circle's circumference to its diameter.*

Are you asleep yet?

"ZZZZ! ZZZZ! ZZZ! ZZZZ!"

If so, then goodnight.

If not, read on...

* I confess I had to look that up as I spent all my time in Maths daydreaming about cake.

When Master Pent spotted a huge
steel ball, he was eager to put to the test
this whole circumference–diameter nonsense. As
he fumbled in his pencil case for his ruler, he failed
to see that this huge steel ball was, in fact, swinging
straight towards him at speed.

WHOOSH!

It was meant to destroy an old block of flats that
was standing right behind him. Instead
it struck the boy. On the head.
Hard. Really hard.

CLONK!

Master Pent was knocked out
cold. That was just as well, as
the ball batted him into the air.

He flew (interestingly
enough) exactly **3.14** miles
before smashing through the
roof of a shed in a back garden.

WHIZZ!

3.14 MILES

DOOF!

SMASH!

CRUNCH!

Master Pent didn't wake up until a whole week later.
He discovered he was in hospital with an incredibly sore
bandaged head.

"OUCH!" he yelped. "My head hurts."

The boy had to keep the bandage on for six whole
months, and looked as if he were
wearing a nappy on his head.

"HA! HA! NAPPY BOY!"
laughed the other kids.

"HARRUMPH!"
he harrumphed.

Ever since the fateful day of his accident, Pent detested
balls of any kind. The sight of anything round was
enough to bring back terrible memories of that great big
steel ball.

CLONK!

So, when he grew up and became a Maths teacher, Mr
Pent was dismayed to find that in St Orb's School ,
where he taught, there were balls, balls and more
balls, each one reminding him of the worst
day of his life.

Balls here. Balls there. Balls everywhere. In the playground, footballs, tennis balls and even ping-pong balls would bounce at him from every angle.

BOING! BOING! BOING!

On spotting one, his eyes would all but pop out of their sockets, his face would go a shade of purple, his glasses would steam up and his comb-over would stick up on end.

"BALLS!" Mr Pent would shout as he foamed at the mouth.

The teacher's hatred was so great that he stuck warning signs up all over

St Orb's . On every wall, door and window.

He even stuck one to the dinner lady's bottom.

NO BALLS PERMITTED ON SCHOOL PREMISES!

NO BALLS ALLOWED IN THE PLAYGROUND!

NO BALLS WHATSOEVER WITHIN A 100-MILE RADIUS OF THE SCHOOL!*

* This last rule was hard to enforce, even if, being a Maths teacher, he knew exactly what that one-hundred-mile radius covered on a map, using his compass and ruler, of course.

Mr Pent would confiscate all balls on the spot. Then he would lock them up in his special ball cupboard at the end of a long corridor next to his classroom. The sign read:

BALL CUPBOARD
BEWARE: CONTAINS BALLS

Over the years, Mr Pent stuffed hundreds and hundreds of balls of all sizes in there, and there was hardly any room for more.

If any pupil dared to ask him, "Please can I have my ball back, sir?" the teacher would smirk to himself before replying, "Of course, child!"

"Thank you, sir."

"Just one moment, if you please."

Then he would reach into the cupboard for the ball, and pop it with a pair of compasses he had concealed in his hand.

POOF!

The air would spurt out like a lazy bottom burp.*

---

* One of those bottom burps that is in no hurry to leave. It seeps out over a period of seconds, minutes, hours, days, weeks, months or even, in extreme cases, years. These ones are hard to blame on others. Short, sharp ones have an element of surprise, and a dirty look at someone close by is enough to deflect blame. So a close friend informs me.

PFFFFFFFFFFFFFFFFFFFFFFFFFT!

"There you are!" Mr Pent would say as he handed the deflated ball back to the child with a grin.

After he'd finally confiscated every single last ball from every child in the school, Mr Pent went further. Now anything **spherical** was on his hit list. The teacher stalked up and down the school, confiscating everything that was round.

Marbles.

"BALLS! THESE ARE MINE!"

A Space Hopper from under a pupil.

B O I N G !

"BALLS! THAT IS CONFISCATED!"

A gobstopper from the mouth of the gardener.

"BALLS! SPIT THAT OUT!"

The globe from the Geography classroom.

"BALLS! BALLS ARE FORBIDDEN ON SCHOOL PREMISES!"

A suspicious-looking pea from the dining hall.

"BALLS! THAT PEA COULD HAVE AN EYE OUT!"

A string of pearls from round the neck of the headmistress, Mrs Staid.

"BALLS! HEADMISTRESS! BALLS! YOU OF ALL PEOPLE SHOULD KNOW BETTER! BALLS!"

It was a **CONFISCATION CAVALCADE!**

Pent was on a roll, which was odd for someone who hated anything that rolled.

Things came to a head the day a boy named Roland, who happened to have a rather round head, faced the full force of Pent's fury.

"BALLS! THE GLOBULAR SHAPE OF YOUR HEAD IS IN CONTRAVENTION OF SCHOOL RULES!"

"But, sir!" protested Roland. "It is not my fault that my head is round! I was born this way!"

"NO BUTS, BOY! YOU AND YOUR HEAD ARE CONFISCATED!"

With that, Pent picked up the boy, tucked him under his arm and marched off down the school corridor before stuffing him in the cupboard.

SQUISH! SQUASH! SQUEESH!

BOLT!

KNOCK! KNOCK! KNOCK!

"LET ME OUT!" cried the boy. "PLEASE! I HAVE EXAMS!"

"NOT UNTIL YOUR HEAD CHANGES TO A SQUARER SHAPE! BALLS!"

Needless to say, this was the tipping point for the pupils at St Orb's . With their friend Roland still stuck in the cupboard, they were now furious with Mr Pent. It was impossible to live under his tyranny a day longer.

The most rebellious of all the pupils was a girl named, as luck would have it, **Rebel. Rebel,** who lived up to her name with her individual take on school uniform...

Hair scrunchies

Skinny tie

Short blazer

Pop-group badges

Graffiti on school bag

Puffy skirt

Chunky shoes

Colourful socks

...decided to hold a secret meeting of all the kids at the school. No teachers allowed. During a lesson, **Rebel** whispered in her best friend's ear, "Everyone meet after school in the park. Pass it on."

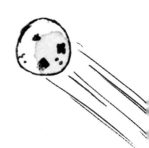

This was passed from one child to another.

Soon the message became mangled.

"Park meat in the school after everyone."

"Meat after the park, everyone in school."

"School everyone in the meat, park after."

However, as soon as the bell rang for the end of school…

D I N G !

…a rushing river of children ran to the park.

Rebel climbed to the top of the climbing frame to address her fellow pupils. The girl was a natural rabble-rouser, and spoke with an urgent energy that inspired all who heard her.

"Have you had enough of Mr Pent confiscating all our balls?" she cried.

"YES!" cheered the crowd.

"Do you want to rescue Roland from the ball cupboard?"

"YES!"

"Do we all need to get our own back on Mr Pent?"

"YES!"

"Are you with me?"

"YES!"

Rebel expounded her plan. It was quite brilliant, but would only work if every single kid in St Orb's played their part, and they would need to play it to perfection.

That afternoon, all the kids left the park, excited about what tomorrow would bring.

The bell rang for lunch break the next day.

R I N G !

As the kids streamed out of the school building into the playground, Mr Pent was on the prowl, as always.

"BALLS! BALLS! BALLS!" he muttered to himself, his eyes darting around to spot one.

On **Rebel's** signal, it was time for the pupils to begin **PHASE ONE** of their plan.

A group of kids began playing football. Another group started playing cricket. Still more played hockey, tennis, bowls, ping-pong or even snooker. Any game you can think of that involves a ball, they played it. As noisily and boisterously as they could.

"GOAL!"

"GAME, SET AND MATCH!"

"PASS THE BALL!"

Except, there were NO BALLS!

Not one!

The hundreds of kids were all taking part in a ginormous trick! Every single one of them was miming!

Of course, Mr Pent knew absolutely nothing of this scheme. How could he? The teacher could see all the kids running after a ball, kicking a ball, bowling a ball, hitting a ball, potting a ball. The thing was... he couldn't see a single ball!

Mr Pent exploded like an angry volcano.

His face went fiery red.

Steam came out of his ears.

His eyes boiled in his head.

"BALLS! BALLS! BALLS! BALLS! BALLS!" he kept shouting over and over again, before he managed to bellow, "WHAT IS THE MEANING OF THIS?"

"What is the meaning of what, sir?" asked **Rebel** innocently as she sidled up to him.

"The entire school is playing with…" He could barely bring himself to say the B-word. "B-B-B-B-B-BALLS!"

"I know, Mr Pent, sir. It is absolutely terrible that everyone would disregard your rules!"

"I know. I know. I know. Can they not read the signs? There! There! There! And there!"

The teacher began manically pointing at the hundreds of signs he'd put up all over the playground.

BALLS ARE FORBIDDEN!

NO BALLS

HOW MANY TIMES DO YOU NEED TO BE TOLD? ABSOLUTELY NOOOOOOOOOOO BALLS!

"Maybe you need to put more signs up, sir?" suggested **Rebel** with a smirk.

"NO! NO! NO!" he thundered. "These nasty little wretches have seen my signs! It's just that today I can't spot a single ball. BALLS!"

"You what, sir?" **Rebel** did her best look of incredulity.

"WHERE ARE THE BALLS?"

"You mean to say you can't see any?" she asked mock-innocently.

"NO!" he boomed.

"That is very strange, because there are balls absolutely everywhere, sir."

"BALLS! WHERE?" he demanded.

"Look, sir! There's one!" she said, pointing at nothing. Pent's piercing eyes followed her finger.

"I can't see any BALLS!"

"And another! And another! AND ANOTHER!"

"BALLS! BALLS! BALLS! WHERE? WHERE? WHERE?"

"THERE! THERE! THERE!" she replied. "The balls are just going so fast that they are a bit of a blur. If you chase after them, I am sure you will catch one!"

Mr Pent passed his leather briefcase to the girl, and took a deep breath.

"HOLD THIS!" he ordered.

"With pleasure, sir!"

The teacher then began charging around the playground, bellowing,

"BAAAAAAAAAAAALLLLLLLLLLLLLLLLLLLLLLLLSSSSSSSSSSS!"

"TWO–NIL!" called out one kid.

"OUT!" shouted another.

"STRIKE!" yelled a third.

Mr Pent was like a dog chasing its own tail.

He went left.

He went right.

He went forward.

He went backwards.

He spun round and round in circles.

He even leaped in the air to intercept an imaginary ball.

"HUH!"

Then slid to the ground to stop another from rolling.

"OOF!"

He leaped on to a ping-pong table to stop a third.

"DAH!"

The table couldn't take his weight. It broke...

CRUNCH!

...and tumbled to the ground, taking Mr Pent with it.

THUD!

Now he was rolling around on the ground.

"BALLS! BALLS! BALLS! BALLS! BALLS! BALLS!" he began muttering to himself, over and over, as if he'd gone bananas.

"BALLS! BALLS! BALLS! BALLS! BALLS! BALLS!"

The bell rang for the end of lunchtime.

R I N G !

Trying desperately to stifle their giggles…

"TEE! HEE! HEE!"

…all the kids began packing up their imaginary balls, before dashing off to their lessons.

"Goodbye, sir!" called out **Rebel**. "I hope you finally find your balls!"

This caused fits of giggles from the kids.

"HA! HA! HA!"

"BALLS! BALLS! BALLS! BALLS! BALLS! BALLS!" he carried on muttering.

A window opened at the top of the school building, and Mrs Staid poked her head out and shouted,

"P-E-N-T!"

"Yes, BALLS? I mean, Headmistress?" he called back from the playground.

"I don't pay you good money to lie on the ground! Up, man! UP! UP! UP!"

Mr Pent scrambled to his feet.

"I am so sorry, Headmistress. BALLS!"

"I should hope so! Now off to your lesson! At once! And stop saying 'balls'."

"Balls! I mean, yes. BALLS!"

All the kids had pressed their faces up against the windows, and were looking on with wide-eyed delight.

It was time for **PHASE TWO** of their plan.

As a still-dizzy Mr Pent wobbled through the empty playground, **Rebel** gave the order,

"NOW!"

From out of the windows of the school building, all the kids started throwing balls they'd secretly smuggled into school that morning.

Footballs, basketballs, tennis balls, ping-pong balls, softballs and every type of ball you could think of landed in the playground.

BOING! BOING! BOING!

They bounced all around Mr Pent. Some even bobbed off his head.

BOINK! BOINK! BOINK!

"BALLS!" he bellowed. Mr Pent thought he might be seeing things as he reached out to grab them. "BALLS! BALLS! BALLS! BALLS! BALLS! BALLS! BALLS! BALLS! BALLS!"

He caught some in his hands, but there were far too many for him to hold. With a look of glee on his face, he began stuffing the balls about his person. Footballs were squeezed down his trousers, tennis balls up his jumper, cricket balls under his arms, a basketball under his chin and a dozen ping-pong balls in his mouth.

Looking as if he'd been inflated, Mr Pent waddled across the playground.

"BALLS! BALLS! BALLS! BALLS! BALLS! BALLS! BALLS! BALLS! BALLS! BALLS! BALLS! BALLS! BALLS! BALLS! BALLS!" he kept repeating to himself as he hurried into the school building.

The teacher was, of course, heading to his special cupboard where he kept all the confiscated balls under lock and key. The cupboard was already jam-packed with balls, and poor round-headed Roland, who was still stuffed in there.

RAT-TAT-TAT!

"HELP! LET ME OUT! IT'S BEEN TWO DAYS NOW AND ALL I'VE HAD TO EAT IS A MOULDY OLD TENNIS BALL!" cried the boy.

Mr Pent fumbled for his key, and opened the door.

"OH! THANK GOODNESS!" exclaimed Roland. "You are letting me out!"

"No!" snapped Pent. "I am putting more in! BALLS!"

Just managing to hold Roland and the wall of balls back, Pent stuffed more and more in.

"BALLS! BALLS!"

Now the cupboard was full to bursting.

As all the kids popped their heads round the classroom doors to watch, Mr Pent put his back up against the cupboard door to close it. It took all his might.

"HUH!"

When he finally managed to close the door and lock them in, the teacher smiled gleefully.

"BALLS!"

he said to himself.

Then, all of a sudden, the cupboard strained with the pressure.

CREAK!

"Sir?" called out **Rebel** from a doorway.

"BALLS! I mean, what?"

"Just one more, sir!"

With that, she rolled a giant beach ball towards him.

TRUNDLE!

Eagerly, Mr Pent pounced on it.

"BALLS! GOT YOU!"

He then unlocked the cupboard door, so he could imprison this last one like all the others.

This would prove to be a mistake.

As soon as he unlocked the door, thousands of balls (and Roland) burst out.

BOOM!

They tumbled down the corridor.

BOING! BOING! BOING!

It was a tidal wave of balls. Mr Pent was swept off his feet. The kids closed the classroom doors, and watched through the glass as their teacher was carried along the corridor.

Roland managed to leap on top of some lockers.

THUD!

He was safe.

"HOORAY!"

shouted all the kids.

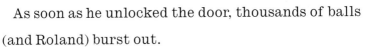

"It's been two days. I really need the loo!" said the boy as his teacher rushed past him.

WHOOSH!

"BALLS!" screamed Pent.

The balls washed him down the stairs, through the doors and out into the playground.

"HELP!" screamed Pent.

The whole school looked on from the main building, but there was nothing they could do.

"BAAAAAAAAAAAALLLLLLLLLSSSSSSSSS!"

bawled Mr Pent as he was swept out through the school gates. He rolled down the road, and all the way out of town. The balls rolled into the distance, taking Mr Pent with them.

The Maths teacher was never seen again.

From that day on, the pupils at **St Orb's** were happy that they could play all the ball games they liked. But they also felt sad.

Why?

Because they really missed winding up their teacher...

After all, why else do you go to school?

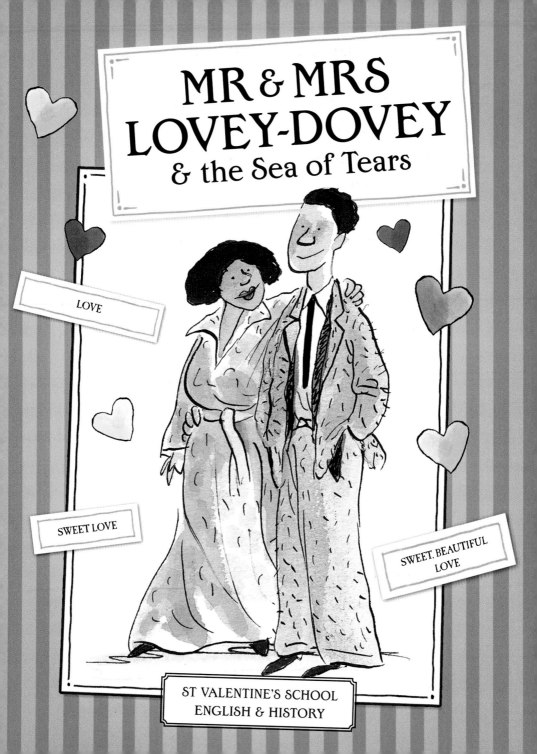

MR & MRS LOVEY-DOVEY
& the Sea of Tears

MR LOVEY HAD taught English at for as long as anyone could remember. He dressed as if all his clothes had been knitted by his elderly mother. Which they were. The man was never seen without his knitted tie, cardigan and tweed suit.

One day, a new History teacher joined the school. Her name was Miss Dovey. She dressed as if she made her clothes out of old curtains. Which she did. The lady favoured floral frocks that went all the way up to her neck, and all the way down to her ankles.

The pair were made for each other.

On her very first day, Miss Dovey was put on break-time duty. Mr Lovey was too. As all the boys and girls of St Valentine's School played **IT** these two lovebirds caught their first glimpse of each other.

To begin, their shyness prevented them from doing any more than glancing at each other briefly, then looking away. However, soon the looks became longer and longer, as they gazed into each other's eyes.

Red and brown leaves fell from the trees around them.

PATTER!

A gust of wind swirled their hair into the air.

SWIRL!

The sound of a dozen violins soared from the music room.

DAH-DEE-DAH-DUM!

The famous balcony scene from the most romantic play ever written, Shakespeare's **Romeo and Juliet,** was being rehearsed in the concert hall.

"But soft, what light through yonder window breaks? It is the east, and Juliet is the sun." *

* It's nearly as romantic as Burt and Sheila's love story in the classic novel *Ratburger.*

In no time, their hearts were full to bursting. Neither could resist each other a moment longer. Mr Lovey and Miss Dovey opened their arms, and began rushing towards each other. They scampered across the playground like gazelles, knocking small children out of their way.

Eventually the pair embraced.

WALLOP!

They held on to each other tightly. It was as if they had been searching the world for all eternity, and now they'd both finally found their **soulmate.** Such was their joy that they both burst into floods of tears.

"Boo Hoo HOO!"

YUCK!

Revolting, isn't it? What could be more vomit-inducing than a teacher in the throes of love?

PUKE!

The answer is simple – *two* teachers in the throes of love.

DOUBLE PUKE!

That first meeting was only the beginning. Soon Mr Lovey was always loitering outside the History classroom to blow a kiss to Miss Dovey.

"M W A H ! "

HURL!

Meanwhile, Miss Dovey was always popping into the English classroom to drop off a cup of tea and a slice of her home-made Victoria sponge cake to Mr Lovey.

CLINK!

BARF!

One day, he ended up eating twenty-seven slices and had to be taken to the sick room.

In no time, the pair of love-struck teachers were calling out messages of love to each other down the school corridors.

"I miss you already, my beautiful rainbow," he would say, even though she'd only been gone for five seconds.

SPEW!

"Until break-time, my handsome prince of love," she would call back.

UPCHUCK!

All the kids at St Valentine's found the pair puketastic.*

* "Puketastic" is a word. Just look it up in your Walliamsictionary.

You might be quietly sitting in the library when you'd be caught in the crossfire of one of Miss Dovey's slobbery air kisses aimed at Mr Lovey.

SPLAT!

Or you might be tucking into your lunch when you'd be met with the horrifying sight of Mr Lovey's face squashed up against the window of the dining hall, gazing lovingly at Miss Dovey.

SQUELCH!

Your lunch would end up being sprayed all over the window.

So far, so bad. However, things took a turn for the worse. **Much worserer.***

The teachers' romance blossomed and bloomed and even bloomossomed,** and one day, in front of the entire school, Mr Lovey got down on one knee.

"Do you need a hand up?" asked Miss Dovey.

---

* A real word that you will find in the world's finest dictionary, *The Walliamsictionary.*
** *The Walliamsictionary* includes it so it must be real. It is never wrong!

"Not just yet," he replied. "Ever since I first set eyes on you in the playground..."

There was still a lot of chattering from the kids in the dining hall.

"Please can I have quiet? I can still hear talking! Thank you!"

The school fell silent.

"Ever since I – Oh, I did that bit. Miss Dovey, whenever I see you, my heart explodes with joyousnessnessness. Please could you make me the happiest-wappiest man in the world, by becoming my wife?

Miss Dovey, will you marry me?"

From his pocket, he produced a ring that his mother had knitted, and presented it to Miss Dovey.

The History teacher burst into floods of tears.

"Boo Hoo HOO!"

"Is that a yes?" enquired the English teacher.

Miss Dovey couldn't speak, so she just nodded her head and whimpered. Then Mr Lovey burst into tears as well.

"Boo Hoo HOO!"

He was still down on one knee, and beginning to look uncomfortable.

"Ouch! Actually, please could you help me up now? My knee has gone numb."

The wedding day was set, and the entire school was made to come. The church, which was beside a river, was only a stone's throw from the school, so there was absolutely

NO EXCUSE.

All the girls were forced to wear bridesmaid dresses made out of curtains.

"HA! HA! HA!" laughed the boys.

Although they shouldn't have, as they were forced to wear pink page-boy outfits, knitted by Mr Lovey's mother.

"HEE! HEE! HEE!" laughed the girls.

Mr Lovey wore a three-piece powder-blue suit, knitted, of course, by his mother. She bawled throughout the entire service.

"BOO HOO HOO!"

Meanwhile, Miss Dovey wore an enormous puff of a dress, that was fashioned from net curtains. It made her look like a meringue.

Although the kids were missing lessons, nothing could be more BORING than a marriage service that lasted NINE HOURS! It was so bum-numbingly lengthy because the groom insisted on reading aloud a ten-thousand-line love poem he'd written about his bride.

You are the angel of my heart.
In front of you I would not fart.
Or burp, or scratch my bottom.
Because you, Miss Dovey, are the one.

The bride, meanwhile, had written a four-hour opera about the groom, which she sang in German.

As the wedding guests began to nod off...

"ZZZ! ZZZZ! ZZZZZ!"

…the weary-looking vicar finally pronounced them man and wife.

"You are now Mr and Mrs Lovey-Dovey."

The bride burst into floods of tears.

"Boo Hoo HOO!"

"I do hope they are happy-wappy tears, love of my life?" enquired the groom.

"I have never been happier-wappier. Boo Hoo HOO!"

Seeing his wife cry, Mr Lovey-Dovey couldn't help but cry too.

"Boo Hoo Hoo! Boo Hoo Hoo! Boo Hoo Hoo! Boo Hoo Hoo! Boo Hoo HOO! Boo Hoo Hoo! Boo Hoo Hoo! Boo Hoo Hoo! Boo Hoo Hoo! Boo Hoo HOO!"

They cried for a good hour or so. The tears collected in giant puddles on the floor.

The vicar looked at her watch, and sighed.

"I am very sorry, but I have a christening and then a funeral to get through today, so could you please just BOG OFF?"

Still the teachers sobbed.

 "Boo HOO HOO!"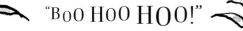

"I said, bog right off!"

The vicar lobbed a hymn book at the elderly organist, who had fallen asleep.

"zzz! ZZZZ! ZZZZZ!"

W H I Z Z !

CLONK!

"OUCH!"

Upon waking, the organist began playing "The Wedding March".

DAH-DAH-DEH-DAH...

Then, when the pair didn't move, the vicar rolled up the sleeves of her cassock, and with all her might she pushed them out of the church.

"BOG OFF!"

Everyone at the school breathed a sigh of relief. The longest wedding in the history of the world was finally over.

WRONG!

It had only just begun.

For months afterwards, Mr and Mrs Lovey-Dovey went on and on and on and on about their special day. They really were two of the world's very worst teachers.

The Lovey-Doveys spent lessons forcing their pupils to watch the nine-hour wedding video over and over again.

They cancelled the school production of *Grease*, and forced the children to stage Mrs Lovey-Dovey's opera about Mr Lovey-Dovey instead.

They cleared all the trophies out of the glass cabinet and replaced them with Mrs Lovey-Dovey's meringue wedding dress.

They threw confetti over each other whenever they passed in the corridor. Worst of all, in assembly, Mr Lovey-Dovey recited his ten-thousand-line poem every single morning!

For you my heart will forever be true.
Without you, I would always be blue.
Blue as in sad, not like as in a Smurf.

So far, so really bad. But things were about to get

badder.*

One day, a **bump** appeared in Mrs Lovey-Dovey's tummy.

"I AM GOING TO HAVE A BABY-WABY-WOO-WAH!"

* Again, you will find this word in your 𝘞𝘢𝘭𝘭𝘪𝘢𝘮𝘴𝘪𝘤𝘵𝘪𝘰𝘯𝘢𝘳𝘺, available at all bad bookshops.

I won't go into how exactly. The bump got bigger and bigger and bigger, until one day there was no bump any more, just a really big baby.

"Boo Hoo HOO!" he cried.

"Boo Hoo HOO!" cried his adoring parents.

That really big baby grew up to become a really big boy. Before long, he became a pupil at St Valentine's in a school uniform made by his mummy – out of curtains, of course.

Now there were three Lovey-Doveys at the school!

Mr Lovey-Dovey,

Mrs Lovey-Dovey and

Master Lovey-Dovey.

Of course, the boy was the ultimate teacher's pet.
He received top marks in everything.

In English
classes, he
would put his
hand up after
every single
sentence his
dear papa uttered.

"Yes, my angel sent from heaven?" Mr Lovey-Dovey would
ask.

"Daddy-waddy?"

"Yes, sonny-wonny?"

"I just needed to telly-welly you that you are the
mostest-wostest wondermental papa-poo-poo in the
whole wide worldy-woo-wah."

Mr Lovey-Dovey would burst into floods of tears.

"Boo Hoo Hoo! I love you sooooo much my heart
is full to bursting."

Then he would scamper down the corridor to find his wife, drag her out of her History classroom, and into his.

"Yes, my hubby-wubby?" she would ask.

"I just wanted to thank you for giving me the greatest gift life could ever offer."

"What is that, please pray tell?"

"This perfect, perfect child of ours!"

Then it would be Mrs Lovey-Dovey's turn to burst into tears.

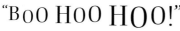 "Boo Hoo HOO!"

"Why are you crying, Mama?" the boy would ask.

"Because I am the happiest-wappiest mummykins in the whole wide world."

This would make the boy burst into tears too.

"Boo Hoo HOO! And I am the happiest-wappiest-sappiest son!"

Then the trio would all embrace, and weep some more, as they were the happiest-zappiest-battiest family who ever lived.

"Boo Hoo HOO!"

YUCK! YUCK! AND YUCK AGAIN!

The Lovey-Doveys needed everyone to know how much they adored each other. So, one morning, they hosted an assembly together. The theme they picked was

ᏝᎾᏙᎬ, ᏚᏔᎬᎬᎢ ᏝᎾᏙᎬ.

As the family shuffled into the Sports hall dressed as huge pink love hearts, the kids burst out laughing.

"HA! HA! HA!"

Mr Lovey-Dovey looked most displeased. "Quiet, please! There is absolutely nothing funny about dressing like this!"

"YES, THERE IS!" shouted a joker from the back.

"YOU LOOK LIKE A PINK WAFER!"

"HA! HA! HA!"

"We are dressed like this," continued Mrs Lovey-Dovey, "so we can celebrate our most wondermental love with you all."

 "Every morning after we wake up," added Master Lovey-Dovey, "we spend a few hours telly-welling each other how much we love each other. So today we are going to share it with the wholey-woley school. So perhaps, one day, you can all be as lovely-woverly-woo-wah as us!"

"URGH!" The whole school groaned. What terrific bores this family were.

"Daddy-waddy?"

"Yes, sonny-wonny?"

"You beginny-winny. Show these nasty, rotten children how **wondermental** we are!"

Mr Lovey-Dovey took a deep breath, turned to his wife and began. "Every morning at dawn I say to my wife, 'I love you more than rainbows.'"

Then Mrs Lovey-Dovey turned to her son and said, "And I say to my son, 'I love you more than moonbeams.'"

Then Master Lovey-Dovey turned to his father and said, "And I say to my papa-poo-poo, 'I love you more than ice cream.'"

Then they all burst into floods of tears.

"BOO HOO HOO!"

VOM!

This went on and on and on. And on. And then on some more. On and on and on and on.

Onning and onning and onning.*

The assembly was going on all day! The

tears flowed and flowed.

Puddles of them formed. Then pools. Then

lakes. The kids in the Sports hall soon realised

that they were ankle-deep in tears!

♥ "I love you more than snowflakes."

♥ "I love you more than rose petals."

♥ "I love you more than sunshine."

"BOO HOO HOO!"

THIS WAS DANGEROUS! There was a very

real chance they could drown in tears!

Next the kids were up to their

knees.

SLOSH!

Then they were up to their waists.

SLOSH!

Before long, they were up to their chests.

SLOSH!

Only their heads were bobbing above

the tears. They screamed for help.

* For the last time, look it up in your Walliamsictionary!

"STOP!"

"HELP!"

"PLEASE!"

"NO!"

"I CAN'T SWIM!"

They climbed up on to their chairs for safety, until the tear level rose and rose and rose and they were forced to scramble up the bars on the walls.

"UP HERE!"

"QUICK!"

"IT'S OUR ONLY HOPE!"

The Lovey-Doveys were in their own bubble of love, utterly unaware of the mayhem they were causing.

So oblivious, in fact, that they didn't realise when the flood swept them off the ground. Still they carried on with their declarations of love as they bobbed around in the sea of tears.

♥ "I love you more than freshly baked croissants."

♥ "I love you more than baby dolphins."

♦ "I love you more than a nice comfy pair of slippers that have been warmed by an open fire."

"Boo HOO HOO!"

Tears and tears and more tears came.

WHOOSH! WHOOSH! WHOOSH!

Eventually the doors to the Sports hall couldn't stay shut any more.

The Lovey-Doveys were swept out of the hall on a tidal wave of their own tears.

WHOOSH!

The three were carried through the playground, past the church, before streaming into the river.

SPLOSH! SPLOSH! SPLOSH!

Still they carried on their nonsense.

"I love you more than double cream."

"I love you more than baby hamsters."

"I love you more than dandelions."

The river was wide and the water flowed fast. In no time, the Lovey-Doveys were swept far out to sea.

WHOOSH!

For the first time in years, **St Valentine's** returned to normal. The school was so much more peaceful without this irritating family around.

However, one lunchtime, many months later, the doors to the dining hall burst open.

BOOM! **BOOM!**

The kids stared open-mouthed in shock.

"GASP!"

Everyone had assumed the Lovey-Doveys had perished at sea.

Oh no.

They were very much alive.

The trio staggered in, their clothes now dripping wet rags, all three of them sporting long, straggly beards.

"You will be delighted to know we're alive!" they all shouted, to deafening silence from the kids.

"We cuddled-wuddled together for warmth!" announced Master Lovey-Dovey.

"We survived on huggie-wuggies and kisses!" added Mrs Lovey-Dovey.

"We survived thanks to the power-wower of love!" concluded Mr Lovey-Dovey.

The Lovey-Doveys were back! And lovey-dovier than ever!

Now it was the turn of all the kids to burst into floods of tears.

"BOO HOO HOO!"

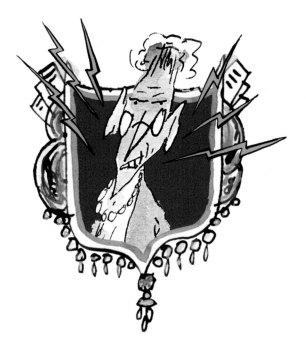

MISS SPICK'S
Trike of Terror

IN A WORLD OF horrible teachers, one in particular stands out for her **wickedness.** Step forward, or rather, roll forward, Miss Spick.

The lady may have been elderly, but she had lost none of her power to instil fear into the hearts of all the pupils at SPOTTINGDON SCHOOL.

Miss Spick's eyes were as black as coal. Her skin was as white as snow. Her tongue was long and thin, like a snake's. When she spoke, her "s"s would be sinister.

The librarian always rode her three-wheeler mobility scooter along the aisles of books as *fast* as it would go.

"ARGH!"

"HELP!"

"OW-WEE!"

Kids had to leap out of the way to avoid being run over.*

* Being run over by a mobility scooter is not as much fun as it sounds, and it doesn't sound much fun.

Despite the wounded children strewn across the floor, the librarian kept her library impossibly neat and tidy.

All the books' spines sat on the shelves in perfectly straight lines in strict alphabetical order. There was never a speck of dust or a spot of dirt to be seen anywhere in the SPOTTINGDON SCHOOL library. Miss Spick enforced a strict policy of

NO BROWSING!

Signs reminded you of this at every step. In fact, there might have been more signs than there were books.

Books were to be taken out, or left well alone. When they were returned, the librarian would pull her magnifying glass out of her drawer and thoroughly inspect them for any damage. Without fail, Spick always found some. When she did, you had to pay!

"There'sss a fold line on the top of page a hundred and thirty-ssseven. **FINE!**"

"There'sss disscolouration on the back cover causssed by exposssure to ssssunlight. **FINE!**"

"There'*sss* a grea*sss*y *ssss*mudge from a thumb or a particularly * sss*tubby finger on the in*sss*ide front flap. **FINE!**"

Spick determined the fines herself. They would vary wildly. The librarian would stare down at your shoes, and determine from the state of them what she thought you could afford.

"*Ssscuffed*, **TEN PENCE!**"

"Highly poli*ssss*hed, **TEN POUNDSss.**"

The money would then be snatched off you, and stuffed in Spick's special tin. The tin was huge, more like a treasure chest, and was full to bursting with **CASH**.

Every child at SPOTTINGDON SCHOOL
had fallen foul of Spick's greed.
Except two. The Tang twins.
Tom and Tim Tang were child
geniuses. The twins always received
ONE HUNDRED PER CENT in all their tests. The
bullies called them "nerds". No matter, these "nerds"
were sure to invent some sort of supercomputer, become
billionaires and take over the world!

The Tangs had been dabbling with all kinds of
inventions already, even though none had quite
caught on yet. They had created:

Internet for cats

Flying sheds

Invisible hairdryers

Self-boiling eggs

Exploding cricket balls

Night-vision goggles for bats

Electric flip-flops that walk themselves

Nuclear-powered umbrellas

Hair-free dogs

Inflatable socks

The Tang twins worked ten times harder than anyone else at school. They were so studious that they had never been told off in their lives. So it will come as no surprise to you to learn that whenever they returned a book to the school library it was absolutely spotless.

Needless to say, this turned Spick incandescent with rage, as it made it impossible for her to fine them. Nevertheless she had amassed a fortune from all the other kids.

But what did an elderly school librarian need all this money for?

To soup up her mobility scooter, of course. **KEEP UP!**

The kids gave the beast of a machine a nickname:

THE TRIKE OF TERROR

It was terrifying with all its modifications:

BLINDINGLY BRIGHT HEADLIGHTS

Snakeskin seat

Parachute at back for instant stopping in an emergency

CAGE AT FRONT
(BIG ENOUGH IN WHICH TO FIT A SMALL CHILD)

REVOLVING NUMBER PLATE
(IN CASE, GOING A HUNDRED MILES AN HOUR, SHE WHIZZED PAST A SPEED CAMERA)

Bullbar

RACING TYRES

Booster battery

GO-FASTER STRIPES

Black respray

MISS SPICK'S TRIKE OF TERROR

To pay for all these modifications, Miss Spick began imposing on-the-spot fines in the library for all kinds of spurious reasons:

Returning a book one second late............. 10p
Whispering too loudly........................ 20p
Sneezing on a book........................... 75p
Looking as if you were about to
sneeze on a book............................. 65p
Dropping a book.............................. £20
Having an untucked shirt..................... 55p
Leaning on a bookcase........................ 25p
Yawning...................................... 5p
Pulling a book off the shelf by hooking
your finger over the top (X) rather than by
pinching the spine with two fingers (✓)..... £8.50
Sharpening your pencil and thereby
disturbing the peace......................... 95p
Sucking on a mint............................ 35p
Bringing a can of fizzy drink into the
library (strictly forbidden)................. £1.25
Having a head shaped like an egg............. 15p
Using a too-scratchy pen..................... 30p
Dropping a crumb on the carpet............... 1p
Smiling without prior written consent........ 40p
Smelling of cheese........................... 80p
Tapping the desk............................. 85p
Breathing more than your fair share of air... 90p
Picking your nose............................ 50p
Picking your nose and eating it.............. £1
Picking, licking, rolling and flicking....... £2.50
Breaking wind................................ £100

Soon it was impossible to even set foot in the library without Spick extorting money from you. So the kids simply stopped going, which was a real shame as they loved reading books.*

After she'd sat alone in her big, empty library for a whole term without one single visitor, Spick thumped the desk in frustration.

BOOM!

Of course, she had to fine herself for doing that.

She took 85p out of her special fines tin, before immediately putting it back in.

CLINK!

Then Miss Spick had a thought.

DING!

* Especially my ones. I have never read any of them myself, but I am told they are brilliant.

MISS SPICK'S TRIKE OF TERROR

If the children would not come to her, she would have to go to **them.** So she leaped astride her **TRIKE OF TERROR,** and rode it through the double doors of the library...

BANG! BANG!

...and out into the school.

As Miss Spick trundled into the playground, a gust of wind picked up a crisp packet...

C R I N K L E !

...and it flew into her face.

"WONDERFUL!"

she exclaimed. That was because it had given Miss Spick an idea.

DING!

On-the-spot **FINES** for littering!

"You, child, that chocolate-bar wrapper you *ssso carelesssly tosssed* over your shoulder will cossst you dearly," she hissed moments later.

"But, Miss Spick, that isn't my chocolate wrapper!" the girl protested.

"Oh **yesss** it **isss**."

"No, it isn't! I promise. I'm allergic to chocolate and have never, **ever** eaten it."

"In the time you have been talking, the fine **hasss** gone up from **sssixty** pence, to **ssseventy** pence."

The kids had no choice but to cough up the cash.

If they didn't, Spick would pursue them around the playground, sitting astride the

TRIKE OF TERROR.
BRMM!
"HELP!"
"NO!"
"ARGH!"

The souped-up mobility scooter had just been fitted with stereo speakers. Now Miss Spick could listen to Beethoven's bombastic Fifth Symphony (her favourite piece of music) on a loop as she terrorised them.

♫♪ DEE DEE DEE DUM! ♫♪♫♩♩♫

All the kids at SPOTTINGDON SCHOOL were running out of pocket money, and fast. Every last penny was going straight to Miss Spick, and they had nothing left to spend on the things that truly mattered in life like:

Football cards   Hair scrunchies   Ice cream

Bubblegum   Rude comics   Whoopee cushions

Stickers   Smelly rubbers   Gonks*

Someone at the school had to do something to stop Miss Spick. The only kids at SPOTTINGDON SCHOOL who were not terrified of her were the Tang twins.

—— It was time for ——

THE REVENGE OF THE NERDS.

One break-time the pair were sitting together on the bench in the playground, getting on with some quiet reading. It was a weighty book they'd chosen themselves to read for "fun". It was entitled *An Expert's Guide to Rocket Science.* Their four eyes

* All these items and more I have been told to tell you can be found in Raj's newsagent's, many on offer, many more on special offer and even more on special, special offer.

scanned the pages, digesting every last indigestible fact.
All was good in the world until they heard the distinctive
chords of Beethoven's Fifth Symphony.

DEE DEE DEE DUM!

It could mean only one thing.

"Oh no," remarked Tim Tang.

"Oh yes," replied Tom Tang.

They looked up from their book. The music was
heralding the arrival of Spick astride the

TRIKE OF TERROR.

"Rocket science will have to wait," said Tim.

"It certainly looks like it," agreed Tom.

The librarian came to a halt right next to them, the
bullbar at the front crashing into their knees.

CRUNCH!

"Ouch!" said Tim.

"Ditto," agreed Tom.

"I do hope you haven't dented my *ssscooter*,"
hissed Miss Spick.

"Us too. How can we help you, Miss Spick?" enquired
Tim politely.

"Well, well, well," began the librarian. "What have we here?"

The lady had a long metal spike in one hand. At the end of it was...

DUM! DUM! DUM!... a burger wrapper!

Tom peered closer. "It looks very much like a burger wrapper, Miss Spick."

"I know that!" she snapped.

"Then we are glad to be of service, Miss Spick," added Tom, and the pair returned to their book. "Good day!"

Miss Spick's face **soured**. "The quessstion isss... what wasss it doing there, right next to your footsssiesss?"

The Tang twins shared a puzzled look.

"I imagine it blew over," guessed Tim.

Tom nodded. "The wind, which is coming from a north-westerly direction, is unusually strong today, miss."

"It is certainly nothing to do with us, as we have never eaten a burger. We only eat food that is good for our brains. Would you care for a blueberry, miss?" asked Tim, offering her one from a clearly labelled Tupperware container.

"Or a pumpkin seed?" asked Tom, reaching in his briefcase for his Tupperware container.

"NO!" thundered Spick. For once things weren't going to plan. "Thisss burger wrapper was sssitting right next to you. There isss a fine to pay. Five poundsss!"

The twins looked at each other and gulped.

"Five pounds?" they asked in unison.

"Each."

"Ten pounds?"

"Hark the geniusesss!" she scoffed. "Now pay up, or elssse!"

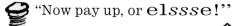

"But, Miss Spick," protested Tom, "we have been saving up all our pocket money since Christmas!"

"For a book that looks really fun called *ADVANCED QUANTUM MECHANICS*," added Tim.

"Hand the money over! Now!" snarled Spick.

The twins looked close to tears as they pulled their matching wallets out of their smart black briefcases, and began counting all the coins they had saved up.

Spick snatched their wallets out of their hands. "I shall take those!"

Then the librarian sped off on her mobility scooter, cackling to herself and waving her spike in the air in triumph.

"*SSSUCCESSS!* HUH! HUH! HUH!"

BRMM!

Poor Tim's eyes glowed with tears. Without a word, Tom offered his brother his handkerchief. When he had dabbed his face dry, Tim studied the back of Miss Spick's scooter as it trundled off across the playground.

"What's that?" he asked.

"What's what?" replied his twin.

"That black box she has fitted on the back."

Tom's eyes homed in on the box. There was an opening at the base of it, like a little cat flap. Every few metres or so it flipped open, dropping a piece of litter as it went.

R U S T L E !

A sweet wrapper... THUNK!

A fizzy-drink can... **PLONK!**

A lolly stick... **CLONT!**

A plastic bottle... **THUD!**

A crisps tube...

It was a **LITTER FLAP!**

"I don't believe my eyes, Tom."

"You should believe them, Tim, because my eyes are seeing it too."

"Spick is spreading the rubbish herself! What a rotten rotter!"

"We must inform the authorities."

"Spick is the authorities."

"Oh yes. We can't inform the authorities about the authorities."

"No. If you will forgive me, Tom, I think I have a better idea," said Tim, his eyes lighting up with his own undeniable genius. "And *An Expert's Guide to Rocket Science* has unwittingly provided the inspiration."

All of a sudden, it dawned on Tom what Tim was on about. They were identical twins, after all.

"Are you thinking what I am thinking?" he asked.

"Great minds think alike."

"They most certainly do," agreed Tom.

The twins smiled, and continued scanning the pages of their book.

The pair were in no hurry to wreak their revenge. The Tangs were methodical, and wanted their plan to be perfect, or, more accurately, perfectly dastardly. These boys didn't get one hundred per cent in every exam for nothing. They read every book they could about rocket science, watched every documentary about space travel and even visited space museums at weekends, until the day they were finally ready.

That morning, the Tang twins spotted the

TRIKE OF TERROR

parked up outside the ladies' toilet block in the playground. The librarian was famous for her long morning poos* that would often go on until way into the afternoon. They knew they would have time to add this latest modification to her mobility scooter.

The Tangs had meticulously constructed two booster rockets. These they smuggled into school in their cello cases. Speedily they attached the rockets to Miss Spick's mobility scooter.

* Long as in duration, not in length. Those are two very different world records. The record for the longest time it took to do a poop is three days, eleven hours, twenty-seven minutes and eighteen seconds. That is held by a Miss Constance Pate. The length record for longest poop is 2.7 miles, end to end. That is held by a Mr Malcolm Mangle. An interesting fact is that the pair met at a Poop Prize-giving Ceremony, and fell madly in love. Now they have a baby who they hope one day will set a new poop world record for distance, meaning how far the poop falls after it is fired from its point of exit.

CLINK! CLANK! CLUNK!

The twins had just finished tightening the last bolt when Spick staggered out of the toilet. They hid behind the bicycle shed. Not being in lessons was sure to arouse Miss Spick's suspicions.

The scooter had had so many bizarre modifications over the years that the librarian didn't notice the new cylinder on each side. She swung her leg over the scooter and sat at the controls.

Just then the bell rang for the beginning of break-time.

DING! In anticipation, she spun the speed dial on the

TRIKE OF TERROR

from "SLOW"
to "MEDIUM"
to "FAST"
to "TOO FAST"
to "PANTS-WETTINGLY FAST"
before resting her hand on the **BRAKE.**

Meanwhile, the Tang twins stepped out of their hiding place and tried to act naturally.

"Good morning, Miss Spick!" they said in unison.

"Oh, it'sss you two idiotsss!" scoffed Spick. "You owe me **MONEY!**"

"We gave you everything we had," replied Tom.

"Actually, she snatched it off us," said Tim.

"I stand corrected."

Miss Spick's black eyes narrowed. "The fine for littering wasss ten poundsss. And in your walletsss you only had nine poundsss and ninety-nine pence!"

"As soon as we receive our pocket money, we will be sure to give you that penny," reasoned Tom.

"We can always deposit the coin through that little flap there," said Tim, pointing to the back of the scooter.

"I don't know what you mean!" protested the librarian.

"Oh, I think you do," replied Tom. "Drive safely now."

"Or should we say, fly safely?"

"What are you two ridiculousss nerdsss on about?" she demanded.

"All in good time, Miss Spick," said Tom.

"All in good time," echoed Tim.

By this time all the kids were pouring out of their classrooms into the playground.

"**Lotsss** and **lotsss** of horrible children to run over! **Thisss isss** going to be fun."

"It most certainly is," replied the twins with a smile.

Spick flicked a switch. Beethoven's Fifth boomed out of the speakers.

DEE DEE DEE DUM!

The librarian let go of the brake. To her surprise the two booster rockets fired up.

"WHAT THE...?" BANG!

But before she could say whatever rude word she was going to say next, fire and smoke shot out of the rockets.

BOOOOOSH!

BOOOOOSH!

Spick rocketed up, up, up through the clouds, lighting the sky with red and gold. In seconds, she was passing through the Earth's atmosphere.

KAB

The rockets detached and parachuted back to the playground.

THUNK!

THUNK!

This left Miss Spick holding on to her mobility scooter for dear life, floating through space.

"HELP!" she screamed, though she was so far away nobody could hear her.

Now, you will be pleased to learn that space is absolutely full of debris. Not just meteors, but scraps from old spacecraft, satellites and space stations circle the Earth.

"Ow! Ouch! Argh!" cried Spick as all these bits and bobs bashed into her.

DUNK!

TWANG!

BoINK!

As for our heroes, the Tang twins, they were still safely on Earth staring up at the sky.

"Excellent work, Tim Tang."

"I was about to say the same thing, Tom Tang."

"I do believe she called us **NERDS.**"

"There is no higher compliment."

They shook hands at a job well done.

"Pumpkin seed?" offered Tom.

"Don't mind if I do," replied Tim.

They walked off together, munching on their brain food, for ♟ CHESS CLUB ♟.

MISS CONCEIT,
the Human Work of Art

MISS CONCEIT THOUGHT of herself as a work of art.
Though with her electric-blue boots, orange hat, yellow
dress, flowing pink scarf and black-and-white tights, she
looked more like a **Liquorice Allsort.**

She taught Art at a school that was the definition of
ordinary: **Humdrum High**. The school was colourless,

except for one room. The Art room. That was an explosion of colour as Miss Conceit had made it a shrine to herself. Pictures of her adorned the walls. The teacher had "humbly" added herself into the most famous paintings of all time.

Here she was as Leonardo da Vinci's *Mona Lisa*.

There she was as Johannes Vermeer's *Girl with a Pearl Earring*.

Frida Kahlo's *Self-Portrait with Thorn Necklace and Hummingbird* now had Miss Conceit's face staring back at you.

Sandro Botticelli's *The Birth of Venus* was renamed *The Birth of Miss Conceit*.

One of Georgia O'Keeffe's flowers suddenly had Miss Conceit's face right at the centre of it.

She became bald for Edvard Munch's *The Scream*.

Vincent van Gogh's famous self-portrait with a bandage on his ear became a portrait of Miss Conceit with a plaster on her ear.

Tamara de Lempicka's *Tamara in a Green Bugatti* was reimagined as *Miss Conceit in a Brown Mini*. Perhaps most startling of all was Miss Conceit's addition of herself surfing Katsushika Hokusai's iconic *The Great Wave*. In the centre of the classroom stood a larger-than-life-size sculpture. It was Michelangelo's *David*, but now it had her face chiselled on it, and was renamed *Miss Conceit's Miss Conceit*.

All that the children were allowed to paint was her! This she would make them do over and over again until they'd finally captured her – as she called it – "immensetal beautifulness". Her poor pupils missed break-time and lunchtime, had to stay behind for hours after school and even missed weekends until these artworks of herself met her approval. It was as if

she were an Egyptian pharaoh, and they were her slaves, working night and day to immortalise her.*

One day, there was an announcement on the television news of a nationwide children's art contest. Every school in the country was invited to take part in the **Children's Art Competition Knockout,** or **"C.A.C.K."**

for short. Miss Conceit was in the staff room when she saw the news. She was so thrilled she spat her coffee all over the headmaster, Mr Dour, who was quietly getting on with his crossword.

SPLURT

"YUCK!"

"YES!" exclaimed Miss Conceit. She began skipping around the staff room.

"DA DE DUM DE DUM DI DA!"

Soon, everyone at Humdrum High knew how thrilled she was.

* In ancient Egypt, thousands of slaves died building the pyramids, which were giant tombs for members of the royal family. FREE HISTORY LESSON!

She **cartwheeled** down the corridor.

She *danced* in the dining hall.

She **limboed** in the library.

She **pogoed** in the playground.

She HIGH-KICKED in the History classroom.

She **foxtrotted** on the football pitch.

She **STRUTTED** around the Science block.

She *cha-chaed* around the climbing frame.

She **tiptoed** through the toilets.

Miss Conceit knew this competition could be the making of her. Now she wouldn't just be a legend in her own school – the whole world would know who she was. Miss Conceit would finally be heralded as

The Greatest Art Teacher Who Ever Lived!

Humdrum High could be demolished, and replaced by a giant golden statue of her!

The rules of the C.A.C.K. competition were simple. Children from each school had to work together to create a piece of art. It could be a painting, or a sculpture, or whatever they chose. The winning piece would be displayed in the gallery of Great And Good Art, or G.A.G.A. for short.

So on the morning that the competition was announced Miss Conceit waltzed on to the stage at the Humdrum High assembly.

"Children, it is I, your humblemost Art teacher, Miss Conceit," she began.

There were groans from some of the kids in the hall.

"URGH!"

They didn't believe a word of it. She just pretended to be humble, as people often do. Miss Conceit was as humble as a *Tyrannosaurus rex*.

Others simply yawned.

"YAWN!"

The teacher was such a bum-numbing* bore, after all.

"As you may have witnessed on your televisual box this very morning," she continued, "a school art contestition has been announcemented. **The Children's Art Competition Knockout** or, for short, **C.A.C.K.**"

"HA! HA! HA!"

All the kids were laughing now, though Miss Conceit had no idea why.

"The prize is nottest money, or fame, both of which, as you know, I shun."

Another groan from the kids. "URGH!"

"For me, the greatmentest prize is posterity! A place in G.A.G.A.!"

"HA! HA! HA!"

Again Miss Conceit had no idea why that was funny.

"Now, I want every single one of you inspirationable magnififunt wondermental children to be a part of this. To make me – I mean, to make | Humdrum High | – celebratedmented on every corner of this planet that we do call Earth."

The kids were not happy. This was yet more work for them.

---

* There were some very serious cases of bums becoming numb at | Humdrum High |. A number of children had, in fact, been hospitalised.

"Do we have to?"

"Not fair! She's always making us do extra work!"

"It's all about her!"

"Can't she just disappear up her own bottom?"

"I would rather eat my sock."

"Wonderment! Wonderment!" called the teacher, as if they had all been cheering her. "Now, I want you, the kids, to shout out and tellish me what you do think our school's work of artiment should be?"

A ripple of excitement passed through the school hall. This seemed like a marvellous opportunity to be NAUGHTY! Best of all, if ALL the kids were naughty, the teachers wouldn't be able to punish them. You can't put the whole school in detention!*

"HOW ABOUT A SCULPTURE OF A GIANT BOGEY MADE ENTIRELY OF SNOT?" shouted a voice from the back.

"HA! HA! HA!"

Miss Conceit's face turned sour. "Properment suggestiments only, please!"

"NO! NO! NO!" called someone from the middle of the sea of naughtiness. "HOW ABOUT WE MAKE

---

* Unless, of course, you are Miss Seethe – more of her later in the book.

A MODEL OF THE SCHOOL USING ONLY FOOT CHEESE?"

"HA! HA! HA!"

"That is not in the least bit funnylous!"

"I KNOW! I KNOW!" hollered a voice from somewhere, though nobody could be sure of where exactly. "WE SHOULD ALL PAINT A GINORMOUS BOTTOM BURP IN DIFFERENT SHADES OF BROWN!"

"HA! HA! HA!"

"You are not taking this seriousocity! This is ART!"

The Art teacher was NOT in the least bit amused, even if every single person in the hall was.

"HA! HA! HA!"

Even her fellow teachers were chortling away. They found her deeply annoying too.

"SETTLEMENT DOWN, PLEASE!" shouted the teacher. Eventually order was restored.

"HO! HO! HO!"

"Good, good. Now, I think we've had quite enoughment of silly suggestables. So, I, Miss Conceit, your humblemost Art teacher, will decidable. The work of artment will be of..."

Miss Conceit left a long pause for dramatic effect.

"...ME!"

"BOO!"

"NO!"

"FIX!"

"NOT AGAIN!"

"WHAT A COLOSSAL SURPRISE!" shouted the kids.

Even the stern-faced Mr Dour, who had been soaked in the staff room, added his voice to the chorus of disapproval.

"What a load of poopy plop plops!" was his verdict as he mopped the last bits of Miss Conceit's coffee out of his ear.

Of course, this is what the Art teacher had intended all along: for the artwork to be of HER!

"Fabulosity. That is all settled, then! We will assemblement in the ground of play, every break-time and every lunchtime, until it is finishedment!"

"URGH!" groaned the children.

" Humdrum High ! Togetherment, we will reach for the stars!"

With that, the teacher performed a little spin.

DRING!   WHIRR!

The bell rang for the first lesson of the day, and all the children began filing out. Unsure of what to do after her little spin, Miss Conceit struck a pose and stood as still as a statue.

That was a strange premonition of what was to come.

After all the fun and games in assembly, at the first break-time the children were set to work. Miss Conceit directed them all from a little wooden plinth in the centre of the playground.

"The work of art will be madest out of papier-mâché!" announced Miss Conceit. Of course, she said "papier" in a mock French accent, even though she could have quite easily just called it "paper". The teacher did the same when pronouncing "cul-de-sac", "liaison" and even "crème". It was just one of the things that made her perhaps the most irritating person on Planet Earth.

"We, well, I mean, *you* will all work togetherment to produce a giant papier-mâché sculpture of me, your most beloved Art teacher, Miss Conceit!"

She had assembled everything the children needed. There were paints and brushes, a tall bundle of old newspapers, a roll of chicken wire and a huge bucket of wallpaper paste.

"It's simplement, children. You have made papier-mâché models thousillions of times before. We, I mean, you will builderment up the

model, and then we, YOU, will paint it. NOW COME
ON! CHOPPETY-CHOP!"

The children groaned.

"URGH!"

They were forced to work all through break-time and
lunchtime, and after school until it grew dark. This
went on for days, weeks and months. Miss Conceit
rejected all their work.

"NO! NO! AND NO!" she would shout. "YOU HAVE
NOT CAPTURED MY BEAUTIOSITY! AGAIN!
AGAIN!"

Needless to say, the children had soon had enough, and
began hatching a secret plan to deal with their Art

teacher once and for all. It all began, as most secret plans did, with Alexina, the tall, thin, flame-haired girl who was widely regarded as the naughtiest kid at ⌈ **Humdrum High** ⌉.

"Miss?" began the girl one lunchtime, months after they'd begun work on the piece for the **C.A.C.K.** competition.

"Yes, now, erm, don't tell me," replied the teacher as she preened herself. "I pride myself on remembermenting the name of every single child at ⌈ **Humdrum High** ⌉. Colin?"

"No!" replied the girl.

"Trevor?"

"NO!"

"Mohammed?"

"NOO! It's Alexina."

"Oh yes, of course. It's a very similarish-sounding name to Mohammed. Pray, continuement..."

"Thank you, miss," smirked the girl. "Well, us kids were thinking. We just can't get this paper statue of you right. We have tried again and again and again."

"And again," added the teacher.

"That's because we are making the base out of chicken wire, but chicken wire is never going to do justice to your immensemental beautiliciousness..."

"Truement, truement," mused Miss Conceit. "Mosteth truement."

"It would be so much more lifelike if we could use YOU as the base."

Alexina glared at the other children. No one could snigger or they would give the game away. Meanwhile, a look of concern crossed Conceit's face as she pondered this plan.

"ME?"

"Yes, you," replied the girl.

Luckily for the children, the Art teacher's vanity got the better of her.

"That is a splendiferous idea!" she cooed, clasping her hands together in anticipation. "Let's turn me into a work of ART!"

With obvious delight, the kids all began tearing off more strips of newspaper... *Rip!*

...before dunking them in the bucket of wallpaper paste.

SPLOSH!

Next, they eagerly crowded around their Art teacher, ready to begin.

"WAIT!" called out the teacher.

"No!" hissed Alexina. "We've been rumbled."

"I need to strikement a pose."

The teacher began trying out a number of her special poses.

First, there was the HOLDING YOUR HANDS TOGETHER IN PRAYER,

a portrait of goodness.

Then there was the

LOOKING OFF INTO THE DISTANCE,

shielding your eyes from the glare of the sun, as if staring into the future.

Next, the teacher pretended to THINK A DEEP THOUGHT

by resting her chin on her hand.

But none of these seemed right.

"Children, what pose do you think best captures my humbleosity?"

The kids all scratched their heads in thought.*

"I have an idea!" exclaimed Alexina.

"Yes, Colin. I mean, Trevor. I mean, Mohammed. DAVE! That's it! DAVE!"

"What could be humbler than a… squat!"

"A squat! What a splendiferous idea of mine!" With that, the teacher slowly brought herself down to squat.

The pose made it look as if she were about to do her dirty business in a hole in the ground. After a few moments, Miss Conceit remarked, "Ooh, it's not very comfortable."

"We will be as quick as we can!" replied Alexina, chivvying all the other children along.

And as fast as they could, the kids of **Humdrum High** began splatting their Art teacher with strips of newspaper soaked in wallpaper paste.

SPLAT! SPLOT! SPLUT!

"Oh! Oh! Oh!" cried the teacher each time a new piece of sodden paper hit her.

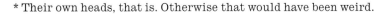

* Their own heads, that is. Otherwise that would have been weird.

Soon, Miss Conceit was covered from head to toe.

"I want this papier-mâché statue of me to be gigantiful," she announced, her voice somewhat muffled by the gloopy paper. "To show that I am a giant among teachers, and I mean that humbly."

"Of course you do!" replied Alexina. "All you want is to be adored for all eternity."

"Exactly!"

"What could be humbler than that? Come on, gang! Let's get this finished once and for all!"

SPLAT!

SPLOT!

SPLUT!

The statue grew
bigger,
and bigger,
and bigger, until it was
as tall as the school
building itself.

The sun was shining that day, which meant that the wallpaper paste, which was really nothing more than watery glue, dried fast.

"Now make sure the statue captures both my innerment and outerment beautiosity. Well, mainly my outerment one!" came a muffled voice from somewhere under all this papier-mâché.

Now the fun could really start! Using ladders borrowed from the caretaker, the children began painting the statue. When it came to the face, Alexina ensured the expression was one of straining, so it looked as if the teacher really were, for want of a more polite expression, laying a chocolate egg.

By the time the bell rang for the end of lunch...

DRING!

...the artwork was finally finished.

"How do I look?" came an extremely muffled voice from inside.

"BEAUTIFUL!" replied the children in unison.

"Perfect! I, I mean, *we* will win the contestition! I will be immortalised in G.A.G.A.! Now all I need to do is get out of here. Hang on! Hang on! I AM TRAPPED! NOOOOO!"

"I'm sorry, miss!" replied Alexina. "We have lessons to get to! We mustn't be late!"

"TEE! HEE! HEE!" sniggered the kids.

Instead of going straight to her lesson, Alexina swung by the headmaster's office.

RAT! TAT! TAT!

"Just one moment!" called out Mr Dour, quickly hiding his jigsaw puzzle under his desk. "Come in!"

"Thank you, sir. You will be pleased to know the artwork for the C.A.C.K. competition thing is finally finished!"

"AT LAST! This saga has been going on for weeks."

"Months, sir."

"Has it really? Well, now it is done, that should shut up Miss Conceit for a while. Very good, child. I will make sure it is collected at once. Then we can use the playground again."

"Thank you, sir."

"Now, run along to your lesson. Well, don't run. Just walk purposefully."

"Very good, sir."

As soon as she left the room, Mr Dour went straight back to his jigsaw puzzle.

What Alexina hadn't told him, of course, was that Miss Conceit was still inside the artwork!

All the kids rushed to the windows of their classrooms when they heard a huge truck driving into the playground.

BRUM!

BEEP! BEEP BEEP!

The statue was loaded on to the back of the truck.

Before being driven off.

BRUM!

"TEE! HEE! HEE!" the children sniggered as it disappeared through the school gates. The kids in Alexina's class all patted her on the back, which made her glow with pride.

A week later, the winner of the nationwide art competition was announced on television. The entire school gathered in the hall to watch.

"The artwork that will be put on permanent display in G.A.G.A. is –" the presenter paused for dramatic effect – **"Squatting Art Teacher** by the children of Humdrum High !"

Everyone cheered.

"HOORAY!"

No one louder than Alexina.

"YES!"

Even Mr Dour did a little skip and a jump.

"HOORAY!"

There was one voice that remained unusually silent: Miss Conceit's. The teacher had been missing for a number of days now.

Then days became weeks, weeks became months, and months became years. What only the children of Humdrum High knew was that their Art teacher was encased in her own statue.

So, if your school ever takes you on a visit to the Great And Good Art gallery, or **G.A.G.A.**, make sure you put your ear up next to the statue of the **C.A.C.K.**-award-winning **Squatting Art Teacher** by the children of Humdrum High . You might just hear a muffled voice from the inside say, "HELP! HELP! LET ME OUT! I CAN'T KEEP THIS POSITIONISH FOR MUCH LONGERMENT!"

Miss Conceit's dream had come true.

The teacher was a work of art.

A giant pooping one!

DOCTOR DREAD
& the Chair of a Thousand Farts

THIS IS A HORROR STORY.

Do you dare to read on?

No? Then turn to the next story.

Yes? You have been warned, and don't blame me if you have **NIGHTMARES!**

Doctor Dread was the most horrifying teacher who ever stalked the Earth.

He was half man and half **MONSTER.**

The Science teacher revelled in his own horrifying appearance. He loved the fact that all the kids at GRUNGE HILL were terrified of him. The man smirked to himself as they darted out of his way.

Doctor Dread's face was permanently scrunched up, like an angry walnut, holding a monocle in place. It looked as if he had just one beady eye, like a cyclops.

He had long ginger sideburns, or "mutton chops", creeping all the way down to his chin. Ginger hair exploded from his nose and ears like WILDFIRE.

His teeth were long and pointed like fangs.

His nose was a wonderland for warts.

He always wore the same WHITE laboratory coat. Except this WHITE laboratory coat had not been WHITE for centuries, as he never, ever washed it. It was so thick with **grime** and **grease** it was actually a deep shade of **BROWN.** There were so many stains on it...

Egg...

Brown sauce...

Blood...

Cream cheese...

Custard...

Snot...

Spaghetti sauce...

Drool...

Marmalade...

Lard...

...that if you dipped it in boiling water you could have made soup.*

Doctor Dread had sandals on his feet, so he could show off his **terrifying toes.** They were a sight that would give you a fright, with their long claw-like nails, open sores and rancid **foot cheese.**

* A soup that dinner lady Mrs Splatt might serve up. More of her wickedness later in the book.

When Doctor Dread marked your homework, it would be returned with all sorts of **nasties** stuck to it:

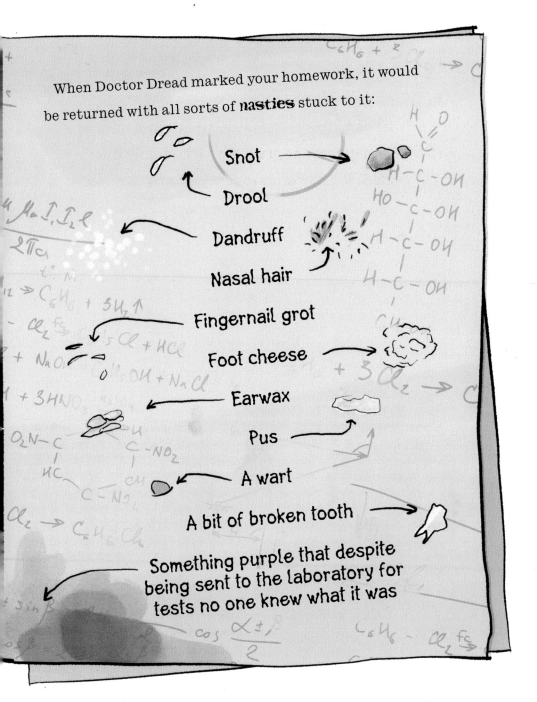

Snot

Drool

Dandruff

Nasal hair

Fingernail grot

Foot cheese

Earwax

Pus

A wart

A bit of broken tooth

Something purple that despite being sent to the laboratory for tests no one knew what it was

So far, so **MONSTROUS.** But I haven't even told you the most horrifying thing about Doctor Dread yet.

His bottom burps.

PFT!

He blew off ALL the time. His trumps were so frequent they might as well have been continuous.

PFFFFFFFFFFFFFFFFFFFFFFFFFT!

There was less time when Doctor Dread wasn't passing wind than when he was.

The slightest movement was enough to make the teacher release his **poisonous gas**...

Sitting down...

PFT!

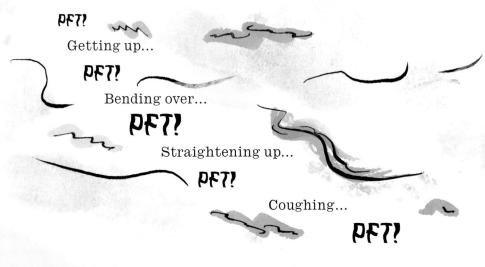

Getting up...

PFT!

Bending over...

PFT!

Straightening up...

PFT!

Coughing...

PFT!

Sneezing... **PFT?** Throwing... **PFT?** Catching... **PFT?**

Scratching an itch... **PFT?** Breathing... **PFT?**

Blinking... **PFT?** Thinking... **PFT?**

Doctor Dread's parps were so strong that they were actually visible. A trail of bubbles followed him around the school.

His chair in the Science room was known as the "CHAIR OF A THOUSAND FARTS". Since Dread sat there for hours at a time, releasing cubic metre after cubic metre of bottom gas, the chair was highly toxic.

Once, as a dare, a girl put her nose right up against the seat of the chair. Immediately, she passed out and slumped to the floor.

THUD!

When she couldn't be revived, an ambulance was called.

NEE-NAW! NEE-NAW!

The girl was rushed to hospital, where she was kept in an isolation ward for a week.

B E E P !
B E E P ! B E E P !

Months later, the girl returned to school, but she was never the same again. During lessons, she just sat at the back of the class, staring forward, silently rocking, a look of unspeakable **HORROR** in her eyes.

So, if one of the pupils in Doctor Dread's Science class did anything wrong, he had the perfect punishment. He would make them sit in his **CHAIR OF A THOUSAND FARTS!**

"No! No!" the child would cry. "Not the CHAIR OF A THOUSAND FARTS! Anything but that!"

Doctor Dread would grin, baring his fangs.

"Yes, boy. Come here," he would say, beckoning as he rose up out of his chair, of course leaving one last brown bubble behind.

PFT!

The child would then be led to the chair, and ordered to: "SIT!"

Reluctantly, they would. The entire class would look on at Dread's poor victim, feeling the bottom burp slowly engulf* them.

"ARGH!" they would scream as Doctor Dread let out an EVIL cackle.

"WUH! HUH! HUH! Right, who else dares to talk in my lesson?"

There would be SILENCE!

* Or "enguff".

One day, a boy arrived at GRUNGE HILL who would become the teacher's greatest foe, a boy so gruesome he made Doctor Dread look like a beautiful *princess*. You might think that would be impossible, but you'd be wrong. That is because you've not met **Bog**.

Bog was a boy who looked like he'd risen from a swamp rather than being born.

No one knew if **"Bog"** was his real name or not, but it was certainly apt. Like a bog, he was damp and muddy. He had worms in his pocket, twigs and leaves in his hair and moss growing out of his ears. When the boy walked, there was the sound of squelching.

SQUELCH! SQUELCH! SQUELCH!

Not only was he gruesome to look at, but **Bog** was ~~BAD~~ too. Immediately, he became known as the baddest boy in school.

Bog never, ever did his homework. His excuse?

"I ate it!"

Which was true. When the teacher became angry, **Bog**

would snort with laughter.

"SNORT! SNORT! SNORT!"

He swiped all the loo rolls from every toilet in
the school. Then he wrapped the History teacher,
Mr Obsolete, in it while he was snoozing so he
looked like an Egyptian mummy.

"ZZZZZ! ZZZZZ! ZZZZZ!"

"SNORT! SNORT! SNORT!"

Next he pinched books from the library and tore out all
the pages to wipe his bottom, even though he never
normally even wiped his bottom!

Rip! Rip! Rip! WIPE! WIPE! WIPE!

"SNORT! SNORT! SNORT!"

He put the wiggliest, waggliest worms inside the girls'
shoes when they were outside playing netball. When they
slipped their feet back in them, they were horrified.

"ARGH!"

"YUCK!"

"NOOO!"

"SNORT! SNORT! SNORT!"

He let the air out of all the footballs and replaced it with his own bottom burps, so every time someone kicked the ball a stink came out.

PFT!

"SNORT! SNORT! SNORT!"

He snotted on the floor just outside the boys' toilet until he'd created a big pool. Then he hid behind the lockers and watched as boy after boy slipped over on their bottoms.

S L I D E !

"OOF!"

"SNORT! SNORT! SNORT!"

He started a snowball fight with mashed potato in the dining hall. **Bog** made sure every kid got hit with a mashball right in the face.

SPLIT! SPLAT! SPLOT!

"SNORT! SNORT! SNORT!"

He nicked a pot of purple paint from the Art room. He then painted his bottom purple, and covered the walls in bum prints.

SPLUT!

"SNORT! SNORT! SNORT!"

He dropped a slippery, slappery, sluppery slug down the back of the head boy's shirt.

"ARGH!"

"SNORT! SNORT! SNORT!"

He tricked some younger kids into swallowing live tadpoles by telling them they were yummy chocolate balls.

"EURGH!"

"I WANT MY MUMMY!"

"BOO! HOO! HOO!"

"SNORT! SNORT! SNORT!"

However, **Bog** would save his absolute worst behaviour for his Science lesson. He knew he'd met his match in Doctor Dread, and was hell-bent on getting the better of him.

If the boy was warned NOT to spill the bubbling liquid he was holding as it would burn through the worktop, he would pour it straight on to it.

SIZZLE!

If **Bog** was ordered NOT to stick the iron filings to his face to create a comedy beard, he would do it anyway.

"TA-DA!"

If **Bog** was told NEVER to mix two acids together as they would cause an explosion, the boy would do just that.

"**BOG!**" Dread barked one afternoon, spraying the entire class with his spittle. "You are in deep, deep doo-doo!"

"What have I done now, sir?" replied **Bog** with a smirk.

"Stuck this piece of paper to my back!" Doctor Dread turned round. On his lab coat was a sign that read BEWARE! TOXIC GAS!

All the rest of the children in the classroom sniggered nervously.

"HEE! HEE! HEE!"

"QUIET!" boomed the teacher.

And there was quiet.

Dread continued, "**Bog,** I have the perfect punishment for you. One that is guaranteed to reduce even the **naughtiest** of children to floods of tears. **Bog!** I command you! You must come and sit in my CHAIR OF A THOUSAND FARTS! WUH! HUH! HUH!"

As the teacher rose from his chair, all eyes in the Science room turned to the back of the class. To the surprise of all the kids, **Bog** had a big fat grin on his face.

"Gladly, sir!" the boy replied brightly. With that, he

hopped off his stool and skipped to the front. Before
Dread could order the boy to $SIT!$, he had already
bounced down on to the chair.

SQUELCH!

"MMM!" sighed **Bog,** his nostrils flared to savour the
scent, like a cartoon child sniffing gravy in a television
commercial. "What a delicious aroma."

Doctor Dread looked lost. "But, boy! This is the
dreaded CHAIR OF A THOUSAND FARTS!" he thundered.

Bog's expression turned to one of quiet concentration.

Then a trumpet sound came from his bottom.

PFFFFFFT!

"Make that a thousand and one, sir!"

"HEE! HEE! HEE!" sniggered the kids.

"SILENCE!" thundered Dread.

This only made them laugh some more.

"HA! HA! HA!"

"I said, 'SILENCE!'"

It was too late. Dread had lost control of his classroom.

"GET BACK TO YOUR PLACE AT ONCE! AT ONCE!"

he bellowed.

The boy jumped up, and with a spring in his step
bounced back on to his stool. The teacher slumped
back down into his CHAIR OF A THOUSAND AND ONE FARTS,
defeated. As if that wasn't bad enough, Dread began
choking.

"URGH!"

He seized his neck with his hand...

"HUK! HUK! HUK!"

...and retched. "B-O-G!"

That stink bomb Bog had left behind was
absolutely LETHAL. It was far worse than his own

bottom bubbles. In comparison, they smelled like the sweetest perfume.*

D R I N G !

The bell rang for the end of the lesson, as a still-choking Doctor Dread slid down on to the floor.

SLURP!

Lying there in a pool of his own spittle, the once-feared teacher was determined to do something, **anything**, to get

REVENGE.

* For your information, the sweetest perfume is, in fact, my own scent, *A Whiff of Walliams*, 99p a gallon.

So that night, when he returned home to his basement flat on the outskirts of town, the teacher limped straight down to his top-secret laboratory deep underground. There, by candlelight, he began devising a host of new punishments, each one far deadlier than the CHAIR OF A THOUSAND AND ONE FARTS. Dread made mechanical drawings on a chalkboard, and began collecting all the ingredients he needed.

Putting the end of a bendy straw into his ear, he sucked out all the yellowy wax.

SWURP!

Next, he rolled it into balls.

Then he placed the straw into his nostrils, so he could extract every last drop of snot.

SLORP!

Dread collected gallons of it, filling three old tin baths to the brim.

The teacher worked through the night. By dawn, he'd finally finished and was ready to unleash these punishments on **Bog**.

"WUH! HUH! HUH!" he cackled.

Dread was determined to teach this blasted boy a lesson, once and for all.

D R I N G !

The bell rang for the first lesson of the day, and for **Bog** it was Science. Dread smirked as the boy squelched his way into his classroom.

SQUELCH! SQUILCH! SQUOLCH!

Little did he know what was coming to him.

However, **Bog** had a plan of his own. Under his desk at the back of the class, he began secretly mixing together some of the gloopiest chemicals in a pot. The boy wanted to make the stickiest, gunkiest gunk so he could glue his teacher to his own chair! He would be stuck to the CHAIR OF A THOUSAND AND ONE FARTS forever!

Little did HE know what was coming to HIM!

With his beady eye, Dread spotted that his nemesis was up to no good.

Perfect!

Now he could begin unleashing his torrent of **EVIL** punishments on the boy.

"Not paying attention again, **Bog?**" demanded Dread from the front of the class.

"Wot, sir?" replied **Bog** as he tried to hide what he was doing. He didn't want to spoil the surprise!

"Exactly," muttered the teacher, a ghoulish grin spreading across his face. "COME HERE!"

He beckoned with his long, thin finger.

Immediately, the boy hid the pot of gunk in his blazer pocket, and **squelched** his way to the front of the class.

SQUELCH! SQUILCH! SQUOLCH!

All the other children stopped what they were doing and stared. What was the world's worst teacher going to do to the world's worst child?

"Here, boy," said the teacher, holding up a paper bag. "Because you have not been listening again, you must

eat one of these jellies from my
BAG OF DOOM! WUH! HUH! HUH!"

Bog peered down into the bag at a collection of sad-looking soft and shiny "sweets".

"BAG OF DOOM? What are they made of?" asked the boy suspiciously.

"Try one and tell me!"

Bog shrugged and rummaged in the bag, before popping one in his mouth.

"They taste a little sour," he remarked.

"That's because, **Bog,**" began Dread, "they are made of my own **earwax!**"

"EURGH!" All the kids in the class were repulsed.

Not **Bog**. The boy rummaged in the bag and popped another in his mouth. "Scrumptious!"

He then helped himself to a handful that he stuffed into his trouser pocket. "I'll have those later as a snack."

The teacher thumped his desk in frustration.

 THUD!

Still, Dread had plenty more punishments planned.

"No matter, boy," he growled. "Go and stand in the corner."

Bog did as he was told.

"I do hope it doesn't... snow!" announced the teacher.

"Snow? Inside, sir?"

"Yes! Inside! As you come face to face with...

THE BUCKET OF MISFORTUNE! WUH! HUH! HUH!"

The man pulled a cord on the wall, which emptied a rusty old bucket concealed overhead. A blizzard swirled down from above.

WHIRR!

In no time, the boy was completely covered from head to toe in flecks of white. He looked like the abominable snowman.*

* Another name for the yeti. Many believe this rarely spotted ape-like mountain creature is made up, but I once saw him buying a tin of baked beans in my local supermarket. Now I wish I had asked for a selfie.

| BEFORE | AFTER |

"I love snow, sir!" exclaimed **Bog.** He stuck out his tongue to sample some. "It doesn't taste like snow, though."

"That is because it is made from my own dandruff!"

"YUCK!" went all the kids in the class.

"Oh, good. I need some spare dandruff. I had all but run out."

With that, **Bog** began picking up handfuls of the stuff and pouring it all over his head and shoulders.

"Fantastic. Thank you, sir!"

The teacher stamped his foot in frustration.

STOMP! STOMP! STOMP!

"If the **BAG OF DOOM** and the **BUCKET OF MISFORTUNE** have **not** brought you to your knees, then this certainly will. It is the **HOSE OF HORROR!** **WUH! HUH! HUH!**"

With that, Dread lifted up a hose that was connected to a huge cylinder concealed behind his desk. The teacher turned the nozzle and shot a **torrent** of **slime** straight at **Bog.**

SPLURT!

In seconds, the boy was covered from head to toe in a greeny, browny, yellow **sludge.** It was mainly snot, but goodness knows what else the bad doctor had added to the mix.

All the kids screamed and leaped up from their desks in disgust.

"ARGH!"

The **slime** was soaking them too and, what's more, it STANK!

"Thank you, sir!" called out **Bog**, enjoying this opportunity to become even filthier. "I haven't had a shower in a long, long time."

Bog began rubbing under his arms as if he were washing.

"I imagine NEVER!" exclaimed the teacher. "Actually, I am going to make it a bath for you now!"

Dread spun the nozzle, and the gunge splurged out at an alarming rate.

SPLURT!

As all the other pupils rushed to the door to escape, the gunge was filling up the Science room.

"GET OUT!"

"HELP!"

"I THINK WE NEED TO CALL OFSTED!"*

Now Dread and his arch-enemy, **Bog,** were the only ones left inside. Both were up to their waists in **gunge.**

"Oh. I nearly forgot!" began **Bog** with a grin on his face. "I have some special shampoo with me, sir. Why don't you try it?"

With that, he reached into his blazer pocket, and pulled out the pot of sticky, stucky, **gluey glue.**

* OFSTED is an organisation of school inspectors. If one day they come to visit your school and you want it to be closed down, all you have to do is this: walk towards them slowly with your arms outstretched, moaning, "All the teachers are flesh-eating zombies! RUN! RUN! RUN FOR YOUR LIVES!"

Dread smelled a rat! This was a **trap.** "That doesn't look like shampoo! Give it to me, boy!"

The teacher went to snatch it, but there was a struggle.

"IT'S MINE, SIR!"

"I SAID, 'GIVE IT TO ME!'"

Their heads c l o n k e d together.

CLUNK!

And the gloop ended up splashing all over **both** of them.

SPLOSH!

"Oh no!" exclaimed **Bog,** trying to waggle his head.

"What?"

"I think we are stuck together!"

Their heads had clonked together, but now they wouldn't unclonk!

"It's not shampoo, sir."

"I guessed that."

"It's the **World's Most Super-Duper-Wuper Glue!**"

"I highly doubt an ignoramus like you would be capable of inventing such a thing!" declared Dread.

Using all his might, the teacher tried to free himself.

"HHHUUUHHH!"

But it was no use.

D R I N G !

The bell rang for the end of the lesson.

"BOG!" barked the teacher.

"Yes, sir?" replied the boy.

"Stay behind."

"I don't think I have much choice, do I, sir?"

"Oh no."

Indeed, he didn't.

"Globule of earwax?" asked **Bog,** rummaging in his pocket for the **BAG OF DOOM**.

"I don't mind if I do."

The two sucked on the yellow "sweets".

The glue was SO strong that the pair were now stuck to each other forever.

So, whenever one of them was trying to...

eat lunch in the dining hall...

play football in the playground...

dig for worms...

conduct a dangerous experiment...

drag a younger boy through a hedge...

go to detention...

write a chemical formula on the board...

play the back of a pantomime horse in the school Christmas show...

run for the bus home...

or, of course, release a bubble bomb...

...they had to do it

TOGETHER.

So Doctor Dread and **Bog,** the world's worst teacher and the world's worst child, ended up with exactly what they deserved.

Each other.

MISS SEETHE'S
Detention Rampage

SOME TEACHERS ARE permanently annoyed. Others are always cross. There are even some who spend their whole day **fuming**.

However, Miss Seethe was never not **FURIOUS**.

There was a very good reason for this, and for once it wasn't the fault of the children.

At ⟩RILE HIGH SCHOOL⟨ Miss Seethe had been the deputy head for as long as anyone could remember. For years and years, she'd been living in the shadow of someone. Someone who had the top job. Someone who would never retire. Someone who'd been headmistress for very nearly fifty years. Five decades! Half a century! It was unheard of to be in the job for so long. At some schools, a head teacher might only last five minutes.*

As our tale begins, the ninety-nine-year-old Miss Stint was just days away from celebrating her golden anniversary as headmistress of ⟩RILE HIGH⟨.

This made Seethe SEETHE!

As deputy head, she was just under Miss Stint. Any deputy head dreams of one day becoming the head teacher.

   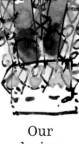

Number one.   Top dog.   The big cheese.   Numero uno.   Our glorious leader.

---

* **HELL'S BELLS SCHOOL for HORRIBLE BOYS.** More of that infamous school later in the book.

But not for nearly fifty years! That is how long Miss Seethe had been waiting to seize the **crown.** Waiting and waiting and waiting. Then waiting some more. Every day she cursed the ground Miss Stint rolled on.

"One day…" she would incant to herself as she looked around the school, "one day, this will be mine! MINE! MINE! MINE!"

The **fury** was written all over her face. Over time…

her eyes had narrowed to become two inky black dots…

her mouth had curled into a permanent grimace…

her ears had begun to glow as red as the fires of hell…

her forehead had become as lined as an exercise book…

and her nostrils had flared so much you could stuff a sausage roll up each one…*

* DO NOT ATTEMPT THIS. IT WOULD ONLY MAKE MISS SEETHE EVEN MORE FURIOUS AND SHE IS ALREADY REALLY, REALLY, REALLY FURIOUS.

Miss Seethe's face was permanently frozen in fury. She woke up in the morning like that and she went to bed at night like that. Even when she was experiencing something pleasurable, like sucking one of her favourite boiled sweets (humbugs, of course), she looked as if she were sucking on a wasp.

HUMBUG

WASP

Miss Seethe had been waiting for so long that she'd grown very, very old. (Not as old as Miss Stint. No one was as old as Miss Stint.) The deputy head was eighty-eight and walked with a stick. The advantage of this was that it doubled up as a weapon. It was perfect for prodding and poking children.

PROD!

"OUCH!"

POKE!

"ARGH!"

PRROKE!

"EURGH!"

When she was particularly enraged, she would swing the stick over her head like a propeller.

WHOOP! WHOOP! WHOOP!

Most days Miss Seethe stalked the corridors of RILE HIGH looking for anyone on whom she could vent her fury. Her favourite thing in the world was to give out detentions.*

Absolutely anything you did could get you into trouble with her. Miss Seethe was known to dish out detentions for the most spurious of reasons:

* A detention is a punishment where you have to stay behind after school. It might be an hour, or two hours, or even more. I was so badly behaved as a child that I am still in a detention and I left school in 1989!

Sneezing in class...

"ATISHOO!"

"THAT SNEEZE WAS SO LOUD IT COULD HAVE MADE ME DEAF, CHILD! **DETENTION!**" she would yell as she whacked her stick down on the cowering child's desk.

THWACK!

Having a **spot** on the end of your nose...

"THAT SPOT IS AN EYESORE. YOU HAVE RUINED THE APPEARANCE OF THE ENTIRE SCHOOL.

DETENTION!" she'd spit, prodding the child's nose with her stick.

"OUCH!"

Humming while sitting on the toilet...

"Toot ta toot. Ta toot ta toot ta too!"

Seethe would strike the cubicle door with her stick...

THWACK!

...before shouting, "YOU SHALL POO IN PEACE!

DETENTION!"

Having your birthday on a schoolday...

"Happy birthday, child!"

"Ooh, thank you so much, Miss Seethe."

"Not at all. And I have a present for you."

"WOW! Thank you."

"My present for you is a… DETENTION!"

"I should have known."

"DOUBLE DETENTION!"

Wearing a squeaky trainer on Sports Day…

SQUEAK! SQUEAK! SQUEAK!

"THAT ONE SQUEAKY SHOE IS CONFISCATED!"

"But, miss, then I will have to run the race wearing only one shoe!"

"PERFECT! YOU CAN LIMP ALL THE WAY TO YOUR

DETENTION!"

Having an egg sandwich in your lunchbox…

"YOU HAVE STUNK OUT THE ENTIRE SCHOOL! THE ENTIRE TOWN! THE ENTIRE COUNTRY! THE ENTIRE CONTINENT! THE ENTIRE PLANET! THE ENTIRE SOLAR SYSTEM! THE ENTIRE UNIVERSE!"

"I am not sure they can smell my egg sandwich on Mars, miss."

"DETENTION!"

Walking too fast in the corridor...

"SLOW DOWN, YOU RECKLESS BLUNDERER!" she

would say as she blocked their path with her stick,

slamming it down in front of them.

WHOOSH!

THUNK!

"But, miss! Please! I am late for my exam."

"You will miss that as you will be in... **DETENTION!** "

Walking too slowly in the corridor...

"SPEED UP, YOU SLOVENLY CLOD!" and she'd poke

them in the back with her stick.

POKE!

"OUCH! But, miss, I've broken

my leg!"

"A pathetic excuse!

DETENTION! "

Carrying an offensive

banana...

"THAT BANANA COULD

EASILY HAVE AN EYE OUT!

DETENTION! "

Even having what Miss Seethe considered to be a stupid name…

"YES! 'MARK' DOES COUNT AS A STUPID NAME! I HAVE NEVER HEARD OF ONE STUPIDER!"

"But, miss. I can't help it! That's the name my mum and dad gave me."

"DOUBLE **DETENTION!**"

"MISS!"

"TRIPLE **DETENTION!**"

"I won't say another thing."

"QUADRUPLE **DETENTION!**"

"That's not fair!"

"QUINTRUPLE **DETENTION!**"

"I think it's 'quintuple', miss."

"QUINTUPLE **DETENTION!**"

And for correcting me you now have a

SEXTUPLE **DETENTION!**

MISS SEETHE'S DETENTION RAMPAGE

Offenders would all have to stay after school in Miss Seethe's classroom for an hour or two, or three, or sometimes even until dawn. It depended on whether you got her on a bad day, or a very, very, very bad day. As a punishment, Seethe would set lines, which the wrongdoers would have to write out hundreds or thousands of times.

I am sorry for blinking. It will never happen again.

I must blow my nose more quietly in future.

I am very sorry I have one ear slightly larger than the other.

I deeply regret stinking of cheese-and-onion crisps.

I will not drop a biscuit crumb on the dining-hall floor ever again.

I must not ever, ever, ever smile on school premises. I come to school to be miserable.

I sincerely apologise for being ginger. I will not do it again.

I am deeply ashamed I was one second late for school.

I will never again sing the school hymn slightly out of tune.

I promise to comb my hair in the opposite direction in future.

However, on one particular afternoon, Miss Seethe was not able to give one measly detention. That is because a  *grand tea party* was to be held in the school hall, and every single pupil was invited. All one thousand of them. Of course, all the teachers, dinner ladies and caretakers were there too.

The party was in honour of Miss Stint and her

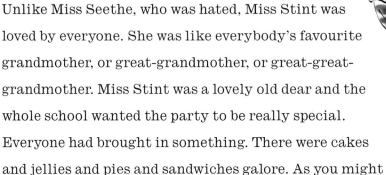

FIFTY GLORIOUS YEARS

as headmistress of

RILE HIGH.

Unlike Miss Seethe, who was hated, Miss Stint was loved by everyone. She was like everybody's favourite grandmother, or great-grandmother, or great-great-grandmother. Miss Stint was a lovely old dear and the whole school wanted the party to be really special. Everyone had brought in something. There were cakes and jellies and pies and sandwiches galore. As you might expect from a tea party, there were cups of tea galore too.

The only problem was... there was no Miss Stint.

The headmistress was late for her own party. Extremely late. Miss Stint had all the urgency of a tortoise. The ninety-nine-year-old was woken up in her

office – she generally slept for most of the day – by her most trusted ally, the school secretary. Miss Epoch was a mere slip of a girl at just ninety-eight. The elderly secretary trundled her boss down the long corridors in her wheelchair, stopping off at the toilet seventeen times on the way. When Miss Stint finally entered the hall, it was getting late, and the old dear had nodded off again.

"ZZZZ! ZZZZ! ZZZZ! ZZZZ!"

However, as soon as she rolled into the room and was met with a loud chorus of:

"HOORAY!"

she woke up again.

Miss Epoch then steered the headmistress on to the stage for her to make her golden jubilee speech.

"I name this ship…" began Miss Stint in her singsong voice.

"No, no," hissed the secretary.

"I do declare this library open…"

"No, no, no!"

"I thank you all for coming to celebrate my bronze…"

"No!"

"Silver…"

"NO!"

"Golden…"

"YES!"

"My **GOLDEN JUBILEE** as headmistress of the school. Teachers, pupils, dinner ladies, caretaker, gardener and everyone else present, who I have not the faintest idea of who you are, welcome!"

Everyone cheered. **"HURRAH!"**

Everyone except Miss Seethe, of course. The deputy head was loitering behind a trifle and slowly turning purple with rage.

"Believe it or not," continued Miss Stint, "I am now ninety-nine years old, nearly halfway through my life…"

"HALFWAY?" barked Seethe.

"…and I have been reflecting upon things, as you might, at such a remarkable landmark moment."

"Oh! Get on with it!" snarled the deputy

head, stamping her walking stick on the floor.

THUD!

"Should I continue as headmistress of  RILE HIGH ...?"

Miss Seethe's ears pricked up.

"...or is it time for me to move on to pastures new? Well, I feel today is the perfect day to make the announcement..."

The deputy head began to do something she hadn't done in a very, very, very long time... smile! Her furious face became, well, HAPPY!

This was the moment for which Miss Seethe had waited the best part of half a century. The headmistress was about to announce her retirement. And, as deputy head, the *crown* would be passed to her. Finally, she would be the top dog at RILE HIGH !

But, before Miss Stint could make the announcement, the old dear nodded off mid-sentence.

"*ZZZZ! ZZZZ! ZZZZ!*"

Her secretary, or rather nurse, Miss Epoch, stepped in. She woke Miss Stint up, as she always did, by gently slapping her boss around the face.

Slap! Slap! Slap!

Miss Stint woke up with a start.

"Oh, thank you so much, Miss Epoch. I don't know what I'd do without you."

"My great pleasure, Headmistress," replied the secretary.

"Now, where was I?"

"THE ANNOUNCEMENT!" bellowed Miss Seethe.

"Oh yes, thank you, Miss Seethe, my trusted deputy and closest friend."

Seethe nodded her head, but said nothing. All she'd ever felt towards Miss Stint was a deep, dark resentment.

"Today is the perfect day to make the announcement that…"

DUM! DUM! DUM!*

---

* There wasn't really a "DUM! DUM! DUM!" sound. I just added it to ramp up the tension. This I have done at no extra cost to you, dear reader.

"...I have decided to stay on as headmistress of  for another fifty years!"

"HOORAY!" everyone cheered.

Miss Stint was much loved, but there was a hint of uncertainty in the cheer. Fifty years? Was she really going to live until she was 149? And still be working?

Miss Seethe looked as if she were about to **explode.**

"NOOOOOOOOOOOOOOOOOOOOOOOO
OOOOOOOOOOOOOOOOOOOOOOOOO!"

she screamed.

"Did you have anything to add, Miss Seethe?" enquired Miss Stint.

" **DETENTION!** "

The whole school laughed uproariously.

"HA! HA! HA! HEE! HEE! HEE! HUH! HUH! HUH!"

"Ho! Ho! Ho!" chortled Miss Stint. "I am the headmistress, Miss Seethe. You can't put me in detention!"

"INSOLENCE!" shouted the deputy head. She was having none of it. "DOUBLE **DETENTION!** "

"HO! HO! HO!"

"TRIPLE  "

The school secretary spoke up for her boss.

"Miss Seethe, please! Have you lost your marbles?"

"YES, I HAVE! MANY YEARS AGO!" shouted Miss Seethe, waving her walking stick over her head faster and faster.

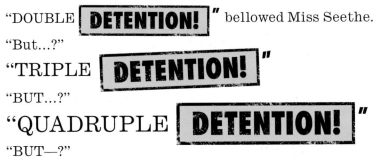

That wasn't the answer Miss Epoch was expecting, but she pressed on anyway.

"Even so, this is Miss Stint's big day! **FIFTY GLORIOUS YEARS!** How dare you ruin it?"

Miss Seethe was a lady not for turning. **"DETENTION!"** she boomed again.

"I beg your pardon?" replied the secretary. She couldn't believe her ears. Now she was receiving a detention too!

"DOUBLE **DETENTION!**" bellowed Miss Seethe.

"But...?"

"TRIPLE **DETENTION!**"

"BUT...?"

"QUADRUPLE **DETENTION!**"

"BUT—?"

"QUINTRUPLE, I MEAN,

QUINTUPLE **DETENTION!**"

"BUT—?"

"SEXTUPLE **DETENTION!**"

"BUT—?!"

"SEPTUPLE **DETENTION!**"

"HOW MANY IS THAT?"

"SEVEN! OCTUPLE **DETENTION!**"

"IS THAT EIGHT?"

"YES. NONUPLE **DETENTION!**"

"NINE. I BET YOU DON'T KNOW WHAT TEN IS!"

"DECUPLE **DETENTION!**"

"KNICKERS!" exclaimed the secretary. "Miss Seethe! You have gone crazy in the coconut! You can't just give a detention to everyone!"

"OH, YES I CAN!"
thundered the deputy head.

"OH, NO YOU CAN'T!"
chimed in the entire school.

"OH, YES I CAN!"

"OH, NO YOU CAN'T!"

"OH, YES I CAN!"

This pantomime routine went on for a few hours before

Seethe snapped. "EVERYONE IN THIS ROOM! YOU ARE

ALL IN **DETENTION!** "

This was a **DETENTION RAMPAGE!**

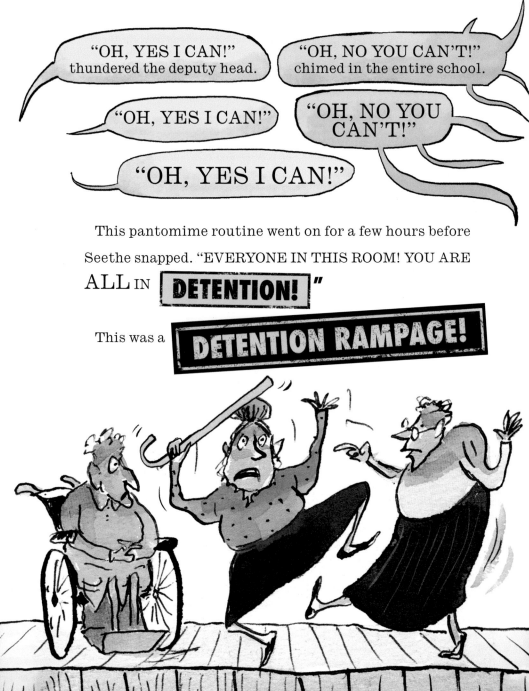

Everybody in the school hall, and it was well over a thousand people, began complaining loudly. Not least all the other teachers.

"NO!" "NEVER!" "NOPE!" "NONSENSE!"

"KNICKY KNACKY KNOO-KNOOS!"

That was Miss Epoch again.

"Merry Christmas, everybody!" announced Miss Stint over the din.

"It's January, Headmistress," corrected the secretary.

"Is it really?"

"Yes."

"Well, it's nice to get in early."

Before anyone could utter another word, Miss Seethe shouted...

"SILENCE!"

...louder than a teacher had ever shouted "silence" before.*

Now she had everybody's attention, Seethe started spinning her walking stick above her head faster and faster and faster...

WHOOP! WHOOP! WHOOP!

* The previous record for loudest shout of "silence" was held by a stocky Geography teacher named Mr Boom. He shouted so loudly that he made himself go permanently deaf. These days, because he can't hear a thing, he shouts even louder.

...and shooing everyone out of the hall.

"SHOO! SHOO! SHOO!"

In no time, she had forced every single pupil and staff member down the corridor, up the stairs and into her classroom at the top of the school building.

The problem was the classroom was meant for thirty, not one thousand and thirty. It was like standing in a packed train carriage at rush hour. Armpits were in faces, knees were knocking against each other and toes were treading on toes.

"OOPS!"

"SORRY!"

"OUCH!"

All the children found this to be most amusing.

"NO ONE LET ONE GO OR WE ARE ALL DOOMED!" shouted someone.

"HA! HA! HA!"

"YOU CAN ALL STAY BEHIND UNTIL THE END OF TIME!" shouted Seethe from the doorway.

"You sad little woman!" mocked Miss Epoch, speaking up for the entire school. "This is all because you didn't get the top job. **BOO HOO HOO!** Now you will never be headmistress. And never get your moment of glory!"

"YES!" agreed everybody else.

Miss Seethe's narrow eyes narrowed even further. Her nose wrinkled and her lips quivered.

"YOU ARE QUITE WRONG!" announced the deputy. "THIS IS MY MOMENT OF GLORY! FOR THIS IS THE DAY WHEN I GAVE THE ENTIRE SCHOOL A **DETENTION!**"

"Not the entire school," observed Miss Stint with a smile.

"WHAT?"

"I think you are forgetting someone."

"WHO?" demanded Seethe.

"YOU!"

Silence descended over the overcrowded classroom. All eyes turned to the deputy head, who was standing at the door, wrestling with this thought.

After a few moments, she spoke.

"MISS SEETHE!" announced Miss Seethe.

"*YES, MISS SEETHE?*" replied Miss Seethe.

"I HEREBY GIVE YOU A **DETENTION!** "

"*ME?*"

"YES, YOU!"

"*BUT I AM THE DEPUTY HEAD OF THIS SCHOOL! YOU CAN'T GIVE ME A* **DETENTION!** "

"OH, YES I CAN! FOR I AM THE DEPUTY HEAD OF THIS SCHOOL! NOW GET IN THERE! SHOO! SHOO! SHOO!"

With that, Miss Seethe held up her stick, and prodded and poked herself into the classroom.

Now there was even less room in there than before, and people started to grumble.

"OUCH!"

"OOF!"

"OWEE!"

"CAN'T YOU WAIT UNTIL THE NEXT TRAIN?"

"STOP PICKING MY NOSE!"

"I AM TERRIBLY SORRY – I THOUGHT IT WAS MINE!"

Miss Seethe closed the classroom door behind her.

SHTUM!

"Right, now, everyone, settle down!" she called out.

"You try to settle down in here!" called back Miss Stint. "There are thirty bottoms for every chair!"

"HA! HA! HA!"

"Some of these bottoms are too large for just the one!"

"HA! HA! HA! HA! HA! HA!"

"RIGHT!" announced Seethe, determined to gain control of the classroom. She clambered up Miss Stint as if the elderly headmistress were a ladder.

"Would you mind awfully removing your foot from my head?" asked the headmistress.

Holding on to her stick tightly, Miss Seethe then crowd-surfed* her way over the top of everyone's heads.

"I AM SETTING US ALL LINES!" she announced as the wave of hands passed her around the room like a beach ball. "I MUST NOT COMPLAIN ABOUT BEING GIVEN A **DETENTION!** OR I WILL BE GIVEN ANOTHER **DETENTION!** "

No one could write a thing. There wasn't room to move your elbow!

"WE CAN'T!"

"IT'S IMPOSSIBLE!"

"ARE YOU BANANAS?"

"HA! HA! HA!"

Undeterred, Miss Seethe crowd-surfed her way over to the cabinet in the corner to fetch some paper. She stood on top of it, and addressed the entire school.

* Not the best method of travel, even at a rock concert.

"I WANT YOU ALL, I MEAN, US ALL, TO WRITE IT OUT A MILLION TIMES!" she barked.

"I AM NOT DOING IT!" Seethe replied to herself.

"A BILLION, THEN!" she snapped back, rotating her walking stick over her head.

"I SAID 'NO'!"

"A TRILLION!"   WHOOP!

"NO!"

"A ZILLION!"   WHOOP!

"NEVER!"

"A GAZILLION!"   WHOOP!

"NO! NO! NO!"

As she argued with herself, her walking stick revolved faster and faster and faster and faster still.

WHOOP! WHOOP! WHOOP!

Seethe was now spinning her stick above her head at such speed that she actually took off like a helicopter.

WHIRR!

Her feet left the cabinet, and she sent herself crashing through the roof of her classroom.

SMASH!

The teacher hurtled through the sky!

OOOHM idoop WHO OOOOOOOO OP! WHM OOOOP!

Everyone looked up through the Seethe-sized hole in the ceiling to see her whizzing through the clouds, still rotating her stick above her head.

"DETEEEEEENTIIIIIIIIIIIIOOOOOOON!"

bellowed Miss Seethe at a pigeon that flew past her.

"SQUAWK!"

Her voice echoed across the sky, until it was heard no more.

"Well, that feels better," sighed Miss Epoch.

"Oh yes," murmured everyone else in agreement.

"NOW LET'S PARTY!" announced Miss Stint.

"YES!" cried the entire school.

They all tumbled out of the classroom and followed the headmistress down the corridor, back into the hall where all the yummy cakes and jellies and pies were still waiting for them.

"HOORAY!"

Miss Stint was the last to leave the party. Way past midnight. The events of the day had perked her up no end. There was karaoke and she treated the school to a performance of her favourite hip-hop tracks.

"MC STINT ON THE MIKE. RILE HIGH, LET ME HEAR YOU SAY 'WAYO!'"

"WAYO!"

As for Miss Seethe, no one knew where she landed, if indeed she ever did.

So, if you find an angry old lady lying in a ditch, waggling a walking stick above her head and barking " **DETENTION!** " at you, approach with EXTREME caution.

Whatever you do, DON'T stick a stamp on Miss Seethe's forehead and post her to RILE HIGH.

They do NOT want their deputy head back!

EVER!

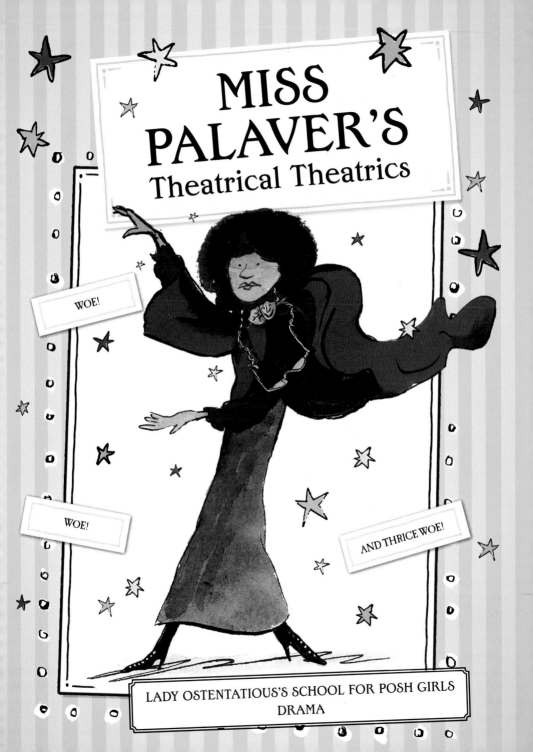

MISS PALAVER'S
Theatrical Theatrics

MISS PALAVER COULD TURN anything into a **drama.**
The smallest thing would make her launch into the most
over-the-top performance.

It could be...

A plastic bag caught up a tree...

"Oh, woe! Poor bag of plastic! Come down from atop your lonely branch!" she would wail.

A teacher sneezing in assembly...

"ATISHOO!"

"Get thee to the nearest apothecary* at once. Ye may only have *moments to live!"*

Miss Palaver liked using language from the time of William Shakespeare, the famous playwright who died over four hundred years ago.

A piece of chewing gum stuck to her shoe...

"Oh, woe! *Oh, twice woe!* I am stucketh to the spot! I will be entombed here for all *eternity!"*

A wasp trapped in a classroom...

"Out, *out!* O stingy foe! Thou art not welcome in my classroom ever! Do notteth forceth me to fetcheth the spray canister of certain waspish *doom!"*

A bird plop landing on the headmistress's car...

SPLUT!

"O bird of foulness, why hath thou smited the headmistress's vehicle so with your ploppy *poop?"*

---

* An apothecary is an old word for "pharmacist".

A girl with a shoelace

undone...

"Stoppeth at onceth

and doeth your shoelaceth

uppeth! Please, please, please do not thanketh

me, even though I hath *saved your life!"*

A book being overdue at the library...

"O book! O book! O pretty book! Flyeth

back to the library on the wings

of a dove! We need thee safely

returned!"

A shortage of baked beans in the school

cafeteria...

"I weep for me. I weep for the children.

I weep for baked-bean lovers of the world.

We must have beans, beans and more beans or we

may as well rolleth into a ditch and die! Die! DIE!"

In case you hadn't already guessed, this particular

world's worst teacher taught Drama.

Miss Palaver's appearance was, in a word,

theatrical.

The teacher dressed as if she had travelled in time from

hundreds of years ago. She wore a long scarlet velvet

cape, which billowed on windy days. On the cape was pinned an antique gold brooch, with the symbol of **drama,** the twin masks of comedy and tragedy.*

Underneath the cape, Miss Palaver wore antique blouses with ruffled collars and cuffs, and tweed skirts that went all the way down to her ankles. Her shoes were heeled lace-up boots, which were last popular in Victorian times. She wore her half-moon spectacles on a chain round her neck. No one had ever witnessed her bring them up to her eyes, so they might just have been part of her costume.

* That was fitting, as her life was a mixture of the two.

Miss Palaver taught at

LADY OSTENTATIOUS'S
SCHOOL FOR POSH GIRLS.

A POSHER school you could not find.*

* It was even posher than
LORD POSH'S SCHOOL FOR POSHOS, where you
had to be a member of the royal family to attend.

The school was set in a grand STATELY HOME, hundreds of years old. There were marble statues on the lawn, chandeliers hanging from the ceiling and gold-framed oil paintings adorning the walls. All the pieces of furniture, even the girls' desks and chairs, were priceless *antiques*.

Miss Palaver thought of the school as the most perfect place for her. She loved the grandness, the history and the snobbery of it. The school was like a reflection of her. She had taught there for decades. Try as they might, they couldn't get rid of her. Over the years, Palaver had directed some "memorable"* school productions there.

* "Memorable" is a kind way of describing them. "Torturous" is more accurate.

First was her infamous **MISS PALAVER'S COMPLETE HISTORY OF THE WORLD.** It was a performance that lasted seventeen hours with no interval. The proud parents in the audience slept in shifts, waking each other up when one of their daughters had a line in the play. If anyone tried to pop out to use the toilet, Miss Palaver blocked their path with a staff. *"Ye shall not pass or ye shall miss a good bit!"*

Musicals were Miss Palaver's greatest love. She wrote one about her goldfish, who she called *William Shakespeare*. The Drama teacher cast the head girl as the fish, who was given a snorkel and flippers. A giant glass bowl was built, filled with water and she was dropped into it.

SPLOSH!

Sadly, none of the songs from **Goldfish! The Musical** could actually be heard as they were all sung underwater.

"BLUB! BLUB! BLUB!"

Who could forget the self-penned play of her own life, **MISS PALAVER: THE TEARS AND LAUGHTER OF A LEGEND**? All those who had the misfortune of seeing this one-woman show tried to forget it, but sadly it was seared into their memories forever. Miss Palaver played herself, of course, from birth to the present day. She was, according to the script, "the most beloved teacher who ever walked the Earth".

A wordless one-woman ballet, AMOEBA,* in which Miss Palaver dressed up as the smallest creature on Earth and pranced around the stage for four hours, was considered to be her absolute worst. The school magazine, *The Ostentation*, gave it the poorest review in the history of theatre. It read simply, **"Poo."**

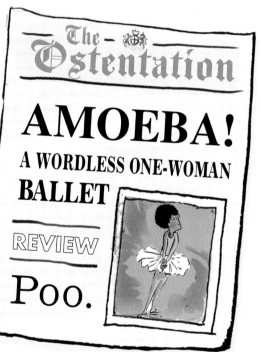

The Ostentation

AMOEBA!
A WORDLESS ONE-WOMAN BALLET
REVIEW
Poo.

* Amoebas are made of just a single cell. The human body, in comparison, might be made of 37.2 trillion. Don't try to count them or you will be there all day.

In BISCUIT ASSORTMENT: THE OPERA, a dozen different biscuits came alive, stepped out of the tin and began singing in Italian. The opera was the show Palaver considered to be her absolute masterpiece. Pink Wafer, Chocolate Finger, Gingernut, Bourbon, Jammy Dodger and Custard Cream were all at war as to who was the ruler of the magical kingdom of Biscuit-tin Land. It was even worse than it sounds, and I know it sounds HORRIFIC.

The most terrible thing that could ever happen to you if you were a pupil at

LADY OSTENTATIOUS'S SCHOOL FOR POSH GIRLS

was to be cast in one of Palaver's productions. As it was a boarding school, it was impossible to escape being in one. Each term Miss Palaver posted a list of who

was playing who on the noticeboard. The girls all called it **"THE LIST OF DOOM"**! There was no saying no. Any girl who did was EXPELLED on the spot, and forced to go to a less POSH school, thereby bringing **SHAME** upon her family forever.

Rehearsals for a Palaver production would go on for months, sometimes even years, often through the night. Worst of all, Miss Palaver would scream at you if you forgot a line or moved to the wrong spot on the stage.

"NOOOOOETH! *You are ruiningeth it!* Now do it again, and again, and again, and again, until you getteth it *right!*"

The poor girls would burst into tears.

"BOO HOO HOO!"

Not that the teacher cared. All she cared about was her precious play, and she demanded nothing short of perfection.

One morning, Miss Palaver was called into the headmistress's office. This was **not** an everyday occurrence, so the Drama teacher's mind immediately began whirling as to why she'd been summoned.

Were her plans for **Drama-themed** food in the dining hall finally going to come to fruition?

Shakespeare's Spam fritters
Chekhov's Cornish pasties
Ibsen's ice-pops
Beckett's Brussels sprouts
Brecht's blancmange
Wilde's wok-fried noodles
Pirandello's pink custard
Molière's meatballs
Williams's Wiener schnitzel
Sophocles's sausage rolls*

* Ten famous playwrights from around the world: William Shakespeare, England; Anton Chekhov, Russia; Henrik Ibsen, Norway; Samuel Beckett, Ireland; Bertolt Brecht, Germany; Oscar Wilde, Ireland; Luigi Pirandello, Italy; Jean-Baptiste Poquelin or Molière, France; Tennessee Williams, the United States of America; Sophocles (they didn't have first names in ancient Greece), ancient Greece.

Was she about to receive a lifetime-achievement award for services to **drama?**

Was the school going to be demolished so her plans for a brand-new thousand-seater theatre could be built, called – of course – The Palaver Memorial Theatre?

Was the headmistress stepping down and Miss Palaver taking over, allowing her to turn Lady Ostentatious's into a drama school with lessons only in drama, drama and more **drama?**

Or, best of all, was she going to be made a dame by Her Majesty the Queen? Dame Paloma Palaver had a lovely ring to it.

The answer to all these questions was a BIG FAT NO. But Miss Palaver didn't know that yet.

The school secretary led her into the headmistress's oak-panelled office. As you might expect from a school so drenched in history, the room was full of leather-bound books, and oil paintings of the previous headmistresses.

"You senteth for me, *O great one,*" announced Palaver as she wafted into the room, her cape trailing behind her. "It is I, the greatest *Drama teacher* the world has ever known! Miss Palaver!"

"Yes! One knows who you are!" snapped the frightfully POSH headmistress.*

She was stern at the best of times. The lady didn't have time for the silly teacher and her even sillier productions. "Sit down!" she ordered.

* The headmistress was so posh that she would have made Her Majesty the Queen look common.

Miss Palaver lowered herself on to the chair slowly and **theatrically.** It took a few minutes for her bottom to actually reach the seat.*

Finally, the headmistress could begin. "One has brought you here today as one needs to talk about what you have proposed for this year's school play."

"The Complete Works of William Shakespeare, unabridged?" asked Miss Palaver brightly.

"Yes," replied the headmistress wearily.

"That iseth William Shakespeare, the playwrighteth – not William Shakespeare, my pet *goldfisheth.*"

"One gathered that. One assumes your pet goldfish hasn't written any plays."

"One or two, but they are notteth great. They tend to go round and round in circles, like him."

The headmistress rolled her eyes. Miss Palaver really was bananas.

"Miss Palaver, one is saying no."

That was a word Miss Palaver never heard. She was such a force of nature that no one ever said no to her.

After the shock had set in, she began her **performance.** Tears welled in her eyes, and her voice began to wobble

---

* Certainly enough time to boil an egg.

with emotion. "But this iseth my *masterpiece!*
This will make me go downeth in history as
The Greatest Drama Teacher Who Ever Lived.

It has never been doneth before! To stage
all thirty-seven of Shakespeare's
plays, and presenteth them in

one evening of *wonderment!*"

"But it won't just be one evening,
will it, Miss Palaver?"

The teacher thought for a
moment. Maths was not her strong suit, but each
play ran to three or four hours, so she began attempting
to work it out. *"Noeth."*

"So how long would it take to stage all thirty-seven of
Shakespeare's often posterior-numbingly long plays?"

"Noeth longer than *a week!*"

"A WEEK!" Even the headmistress was flabbergasted.

"It could be longer, if thou so wisheth. I could includeth
Shakespeare's sonnets."*

"NO!" bellowed the headmistress. She was losing her
patience now.

---

* Sonnets are poems of fourteen lines. Still too long for some.

"Noeth to the sonnets, but *yeseth* to the thirty-seven plays?" asked Miss Palaver hopefully.

"NOOO!"

"Noeth?"

"YESETH! IT'S A NOETH! One means, 'Yes, it is a no!' And, Miss Palaver, henceforth one has decreed that there will be no more school plays ever."

The teacher was, for once, stunned into silence.

"They bring only misery to those who are in them, and even greater misery to those who have to sit through them. One has consulted with the school council, and all the girls here want your theatre room converted for badminton practice."

"BADMINTON PRACTICETH?" Miss Palaver couldn't believe her ears. This was an insult of epic proportions. "Headmistresseth, do I hear thee correctly? Art thou sayething *noeth* to the very first staging of all thirty-seven of Shakespeare's plays so the girls can hitteth a –" she could barely bring herself to say it – *"shuttlecock?"*

"Yes, I am," replied the headmistress. "Now, Miss Palaver, one has an extremely POSH school to run. Good day!" With that, she stood, and showed the teacher the door.

Miss Palaver remained sitting, and stared straight ahead.

"Miss Palaver? MISS PALAVER?" The headmistress waved her hand in front of the lady's eyes, but there was no response.

"Woe, woe and *thrice woe!*" whispered the teacher to herself. It sounded like the first crackle of the thunder you hear when a storm is brewing.

"Miss Palaver? Please don't make a **drama** out of this!"

"WOOOOOOOOOOE!"

she wailed in reply. The sound was so piercing that the glass in the windows exploded.

SHATTER!

MISS PALAVER'S THEATRICAL THEATRICS

The oil paintings fell off the walls.

THUD! THUD! THUD!

And the leather-bound books
flew off the shelves.

CLUMP! CLUMP! CLUMP!

"Stop that wailing at once, Miss

Palaver!" ordered the headmistress.

"OUT! OUT! OUT!"

She began shooing the teacher from her office.

"SHOO! SHOO! SHOO!"

Miss Palaver staggered across the hallway, her cape

fluttering behind her. She came to rest between two

giant columns.

"WOOOOOOOOOOOOOOOOE!"

she wailed, even louder than before.

It was so loud that the old school

building began to

crumble.

RUMBLE!   RUMBLE!

RUMBLE!

A chandelier crashed down from the ceiling.

W H O O S H !

SMASH!

Plaster exploded from the walls.

KABOOM!

Doors flew off their hinges.

THUD! THUD! THUD!

Girls and teachers began

streaming out of their classrooms.

"AAAHHH!"

"NOOO!"

"HELP!"

Everyone escaped to the safety of the lawn, leaving

Miss Palaver wailing alone in the school building.

"woOOOOOOOO

This time she pushed with all her strength against the two giant columns. Huge cracks began shooting across them.

CRACK! CRUCK! CROCK!

OOOE!"

As the columns crumbled, so did the old stately home itself. The ceiling caved in, the walls caved in, everything that could have caved in caved in.*

CRUMBLE!

CROMBLE!

CRIMBLE!

BOOM! BASH! SMASH!

Soon, the historic

LADY OSTENTATIOUS'S SCHOOL FOR POSH GIRLS

was nothing but a pile of rubble.

A cloud of dust covered everyone and everything.

COUGH!

SPLUTTER!

GASP!

* If there had been a cave, that would have caved in too.

As the dust slowly cleared, all the staff and pupils began to make out a lone figure amongst the rubble. The figure looked like a statue, standing motionless, covered from head to toe in grey dust and debris.

"MISS PALAVER!" called out the headmistress.

On hearing her name, the statue came to life. She asked hopefully,

"Howeth about I just direct *thirty-six* of Shakespeare's plays?"

THE
INCREDIBLE
BULK

MR BULK WAS AN enormous oaf of a man, as wide
as he was tall – like a hot-air balloon in a tracksuit.
The teacher wore a tracksuit to school every day, but
not because he exerted himself in any way. No, it was
because he taught Sports.

And Sports teachers have to wear tracksuits even if they are less active than a sloth.

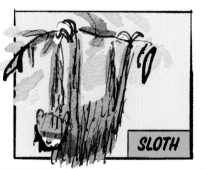

SLOTH

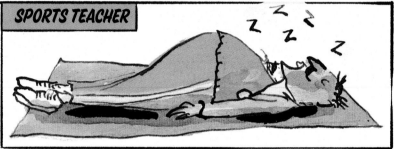

SPORTS TEACHER

Bulk had a different-coloured one for each day of the week.

Monday:
flamingo pink...

Tuesday:
electric blue...

Wednesday:
deep purple...

Thursday:
canary yellow...

Friday:
postbox red...

To complete his look, he had a bushy moustache, a mullet haircut and a huge gold medallion nestling on his hairy chest. Mr Bulk thought he was the coolest teacher around. Sadly, no one agreed. All the boys at TWADDLE SCHOOL laughed at him behind his back.

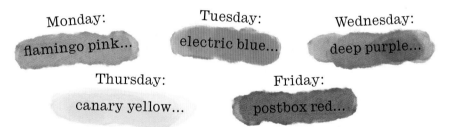

"HA! HA! HA!"

They had a nickname for him that had been passed from generation to generation.

THE INCREDIBLE BULK

It was cruel, but he certainly loved his food. The teacher always had something big and meaty on the go. A million sausage rolls later, he was ginormous. Now, despite not having the appearance of a natural athlete, Mr Bulk would spend the whole of his lessons making wild boasts about his sporting achievements.

"I could have won the Wimbledon tennis championships," he would tell his pupils as he devoured a pork pie. "Even the doubles, playing on my own. Two against one. I am that good. Game, set and match!

DOOSH!"

"The England football team begged me to be captain for the World Cup Final. But I am on playground duties on Fridays so I couldn't make it. he proclaimed as he sprayed Cornish pasty crumbs all over the kids.

SPLIT! SPLAT! SPLUT!

"The problem is I am actually too good at boxing. If I got in the ring with the heavyweight champion of the world, it would be all over in one second! I would knock him out with a single punch. **BOOM!"** he would brag as he polished off a battered sausage.

"I am actually banned from playing rugby at international level as it wasn't fair on all the other players. They would just get trampled underfoot by me as I scored goal after goal. I mean TRY!

DOOF!"

He always liked to end with a big shout even if it meant
the meatball he was munching shot out of
his mouth and hit a kid bang in the eye.

"Basketball is my number-one sport. I can shoot a hoop
from a distance of a mile. With my eyes closed. And my
hands tied behind my back. That's why you won't see me
playing professional basketball. It is so easy for me it's
BORING!

he would crow as he chomped
on two sausage rolls at once.

"CHOMP! CHUMP!"

Now of course the kids at TWADDLE SCHOOL didn't
believe a word of all this nonsense. When he finished a
story, they would roll their eyes – the only exercise
they got.

One day, a boy asked, "If you are so brilliant at all these
sports, sir, why are you teaching here at TWADDLE ? This
school has never won a thing!"

It was true. TWADDLE SCHOOL had a trophy cabinet that was empty of all trophies. It really was just a cabinet.

"Because I'm going to bring home the gold for the school!" Bulk replied as he bit down on his bacon sandwich and squirted brown sauce over the boy. SPLURGE! "YUCK!"

Bacon sandwiches were one of Bulk's favourites, but he loved all the food that was served in the school canteen –

sausage rolls,  toad-in-the-hole, meatballs,

spam fritters,   beef Wellington, liver and bacon –

except... vegetables.

He point-blank refused to eat any.

"VEGETABLES ARE FOR LOSERS," was one of his mottos.

"FRUIT IS FOR WIMPS," was another.*

Mr Bulk even carried around a dog-eared note, supposedly from his mother, in case the dinner lady pressed him to eat any of either.

* Mr Bulk thought the "five-a-day" rule for eating fruit and vegetables referred to five different types of salami.

Dear ~~Diner~~ Dinner Lady,

Please can you excuze me, I mean my son, Mr Bulk, from any froot or vegartables. I, I mean he, ~~is allerjic alergick algejick~~ doesn't like them and may well cry if I, I mean, he has to eat any. They taste yucky.

Yours thankingly,

Mr Bulk's mum

Mr Bulk may not have troubled with the fruit or vegetables (even if he couldn't, I mean his mum couldn't, spell them), but the pupils and teachers would still run to the school canteen at lunchtime.

BRING! sounded the bell at noon. It was like the starting pistol being fired. The race would begin.

"GO! GO! GO!"

"RUN!"

"GET THERE BEFORE THE INCREDILBE BULK SCOFFS THE LOT!"

It would be a STAMPEDE.

STOMP! STOMP! STOMP!

They had to get in quick or Bulk would have polished off the main course before they even got there! The teacher would pick up the entire tray of spaghetti bolognese or whatever was on the menu that day.

Then he would waddle over to his table...

WADDLE! WUDDLE! WIDDLE!

slam the tray down...

DUNK!

...before burying his face in it.

He didn't believe in using cutlery.

"CUTLERY IS FOR QUITTERS!" was another one of his mottos.

Mr Bulk ate like a farm animal at a trough, barely coming up for air.

"GOBBLE! GOBBLE! GOBBLE!"

When he finally did come up for air, his face would be covered in food.

BEFORE

AFTER

He would then belch loudly.

 PONG!

Bulk had the MEATIEST burps. They were so meaty you could slice them with a carving knife.

Then the teacher would move on to the desserts...

"GOBBLE! GOBBLE! GOBBLE!"

PONG!

...before finally devouring an enormous meat-based packed lunch that his mum had made for him. A whole roast hog, a metre of salami, and a hundred chicken legs.

"GOBBLE! GOBBLE! GOBBLE!"

PONG!

His excuse for eating like  this? "Us athletes need all the energy we can get. I wouldn't want to waste away!" he would say as he slapped his big, fat tummy...

SLAP!

WIBBLE! WOBBLE! WUBBLE!

...and waddled off.

After his two lunches, he would crash out on a crash mat in the Sports hall, and snooze for the rest of the afternoon.

Bulk's eating may have been prodigious, but his teaching was not. His Sports lessons were a complete joke. What made matters worse was that a huge match with a rival school was looming, and not a single boy at TWADDLE SCHOOL had received a moment's football coaching. They hadn't even seen a ball, let alone kicked one!

It was the **SCHOOLS' FOOTBALL CHAMPIONSHIPS**, and the Twaddle team was heading for yet another DISASTER!

Every week, the boys would plead, "Please, please, please, please can we have a practice game, sir? Otherwise we are going to get thrashed!"

"Have I ever told you my story about the world badminton championships? I hit the shuttlecock so hard it shot up into outer space!"

"YES, SIR!" chimed the boys. "A MILLION TIMES!"

The days, weeks and months passed and the **SCHOOLS' FOOTBALL CHAMPIONSHIPS** were edging nearer.

In the time when the boys should have been honing their football skills, Bulk was boring the life out of them with his stories about how he could...

...beat anyone in a swimming race across the English Channel even though he still had to wear armbands...

...get a hole-in-one at a golf course in Scotland, even if he teed up the ball in Ireland...

...outrun the fastest man in the world over a hundred metres, and still have time to stop for a kebab on the way...

...karate-kick a tree over...

...win the Tour de France on his mum's three-wheeler...

...wrestle a man to the ground while still eating a bag of pork scratchings...

...weightlift the entire Science block, including the hefty laboratory technician, Mrs Chafe...

...pole-vault over the main school building using only a thirty-centimetre ruler for a pole...

Finally, the day of the big match came. TWADDLE SCHOOL was facing a team from the reigning champions, COARSE COLLEGE. They had won the

SCHOOLS' FOOTBALL CHAMPIONSHIPS

every year for a staggering one hundred years. It was hardly surprising, as they always cheated.

First, although this was an under-twelves match, most of the COARSE COLLEGE team looked much, much older. One even had a shave just before kick-off.

WHIRR!

COARSE COLLEGE TEAM

Second, COARSE COLLEGE played DIRTY.

They spent more time tripping you up...

elbowing you in the eye...

THUD!

WHACK!

or kneeing you in the groin...

DOING!

than they ever did kicking a football.

BOOT!

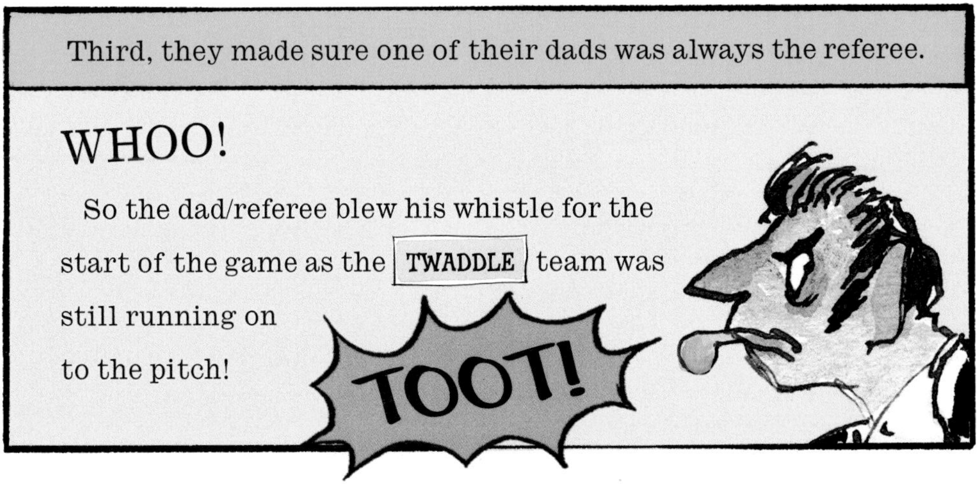

Third, they made sure one of their dads was always the referee.

WHOO!

So the dad/referee blew his whistle for the start of the game as the | TWADDLE | team was still running on to the pitch!

TOOT!

"TO ME!" shouted the COARSE captain, who actually had a beard. His team fanned out behind him. It looked as if there had been a mass escape from the local prison. There was a sea of broken noses, tattoos and hairy legs.

Needless to say, they demolished their opponents in seconds.

The poor Twaddles did their best, but they didn't stand a chance, not least because they'd had zero opportunity to practise.

At half-time the referee blew his whistle.

The score was **10** **0** to COARSE COLLEGE! **TOOT!**

Not that Mr Bulk had paid much attention to the game. He was much more interested in the table of sandwiches that had been laid out for all the boys to eat after the match. Sadly for them, Bulk had eaten them all, except one final Coronation-chicken sandwich. The teacher was now eyeing up the table, wondering if wood tasted nice.

What was left of the TWADDLE team hobbled over to him.

"Mr Bulk, we are being thrashed!" began the captain. "What are we going to do?"

The teacher stood perfectly still, save for one part of his body. His mouth. He was chewing, and finally he swallowed that last sandwich.

GULP! "BURP!"

PONG-A-WONG-A-WOO-WAH!

That was a spicy one.

Finally, he spoke.

"Boys, listen to me, I am the champion of champions!"

"NO! YOU

LISTEN TO ME!" snapped the captain. "YOU ARE A CHAMPION OF NOTHING! YOU MADE IT ALL UP!"

"IT'S ALL NONSENSE!" added the goalie.

"THE ONLY BALL I'VE EVER SEEN YOU CATCH IS A MEATBALL!" stated the centre forward.

"HA! HA! HA!"

The team all laughed at their teacher, who became sad. He took a deep breath, and began speaking slowly and softly.

"I am not stupid. I know what you all call me behind my back. The Incredible Bulk! Well, it's not my fault I love my food. And I can dream, can't I?"

All of a sudden, the boys felt terrible for mocking him, and gazed down at their football boots.

"I know that one day I can be the **GOAT.**"

"The what?" asked the captain.

"G.O.A.T. Stands for **greatest of all time!** And that day... is TODAY!"

With that, Bulk waddled on to the pitch.

WADDLE! WUDDLE! WIDDLE!

"Now we're really done for," remarked the TWADDLE captain. He and his teammates stayed on the sidelines as the COARSE COLLEGE boys, if they could indeed be called boys, all jeered at Mr Bulk, as if to say, "Who is this huge lump?"

"HUH! HUH! HUH!"

However, when their team captain tried to weave round him with the ball, Bulk simply stuck his huge tummy out, and…

BOOM!

The boy/man didn't stand a chance. He bounced against Bulk's bulk so hard...

BOING!

...that he shot up into the air.

ZOOM!

The COARSE captain landed on the far side of the pitch in a puddle of mud.

SPLAT!

SQUELCH!

"One down!" called out Bulk.

The referee blew his whistle...

TOOOOOOOOOT!

...and pulled out a red card to send the Sports teacher off.

"How dare you? That's my son! He's only just turned thirty!" screamed the referee.

"Oh, I do dare," replied Bulk. "I DO!"

With that, Bulk bashed into the referee with his tummy.

BOINK!

"ARGH!"

It sent the referee soaring into the sky. He ended up on a church roof, with the spire poking into his bottom.*

"OUCH!"

Just then, one of COARSE COLLEGE's super-fast strikers took possession of the ball. He was actually carrying it.**

Just as he was about to drop it to his feet and shoot for the goal, Bulk waddled into his way. The striker ran SLAP BANG into the teacher's tummy.

"OOF!" WOBBLE! **BOINK!**

He zoomed

through the air...

WHOOSH!

...before

whizzing past his own

goalkeeper and hitting

the back of the net.

* A spire is one of the most painful things that can poke into your bottom. Others include a cactus, a hedgehog and a medieval flail, none of which I would recommend.

** I am no expert, but as far as I know this is against the rules of football.

shouted Bulk
triumphantly, though
technically it wasn't.

The TWADDLE team
cheered anyway.

"HOORAY!"

The head of COARSE
COLLEGE, Mr Gnash,
clomped on to the pitch.

CLOMP! CLOMP! CLOMP!

He rolled up his sleeves and lifted up his fists as if he
were spoiling for a fight.

"WHAT ON EARTH DO YOU THINK YOU ARE DOING,
MAN?" he demanded.

"THIS!" replied Bulk with a grin, bashing his tummy
into him.

WOBBLE!  "ARGH!"

Bulk sent the man soaring over
the crowd of spectators.

WHIZZ!

Gnash flew head first into a tree...

DOINK!

...and was knocked out cold.

He slid down the trunk, hitting each and every branch on the way down.

DOINK! DOINK! DOINK!
DOINK! DOINK!

Mr Gnash landed in a crumpled heap on the grass.

SLUMP!

"DOOSH!" exclaimed Bulk. "Who's next?"

Trembling with fear, the COARSE COLLEGE team dashed back to the far end of the pitch. Except for one, the brawniest of the lot, who stepped towards Bulk. He handed his pint of beer to one of his team-mates, and stared at the Sports teacher.

"I ain't scared of you, big man!" he growled in his deep, manly voice. He was actually so old that he'd gone completely bald. He had tattoos on his knuckles spelling out the words "HATE" and "HATE".

Bulk smiled. "COME ON, THEN, LITTLE ONE!"

Baldy* booted the ball hard.

BOOF!

WHIZZ!

Then chased it across the pitch.

STOMP! STOMP! STOMP!

Bulk took a few waddles backwards towards the TWADDLE goal.

WADDLE! WUDDLE! WIDDLE!

The Sports teacher was so wide he all but blocked out the entire goal.

With nowhere else to go, Baldy raced SLAP BANG into the Bulk's humongous tummy.

WOBBLE!

BOINK!

* "Baldy" is an unkind nickname, but it was that or "Slaphead".

He was launched high into the air like a space rocket.

ZOOM!

His bald head glowed red he was travelling so fast.

SIZZLE!

Of course, as Isaac Newton's law of gravity* taught us, what goes up must come down, and come down he did.

BISH!

A fourth crashed through the sandwich table.

CRASH!

SPLAT!

A fifth came to rest in a puddle.

THUNK!

A third smashed through a fence.

CRUNCH!

Another landed on top of the school minibus.

* An apple fell from a tree on to Isaac's head, which led him to invent his theory of gravity. Thank goodness it wasn't the tree that fell on him, or we would all still be floating in space.

"What are you waiting for, TWADDLE?" called out Mr Bulk.

His team flooded on to the pitch. Huffing and puffing, Bulk waddled all the way to COARSE's goal. This really was his day, and he wanted all the glory. Leaning against the bar to get his breath back, he ordered, "PASS IT TO ME!"

The boy did so, and Bulk gently tapped the ball over the line.

"GOAL!" he exclaimed.

The Sports teacher had never looked happier.

"TO ME!"

The TWADDLE team did as they were told.

To absolutely nobody's surprise, a second goal was scored.

GOAL!

And another. **GOAL!**

And another. **GOAL!**

And another. **GOAL!**

Soon, the teacher had scored hundreds of goals. Most he didn't even kick, they just rebounded off his big, fat foot. It was hard to keep count of all the goals, but the referee did his best from atop the church spire, and he called out, "397!"

As he blew his whistle for the end of the match…

…Bulk began a victory lap round the pitch. The teacher was now too puffed out even to waddle, so instead he ordered the TWADDLE team to:

"CARRY ME!"

"You what, sir?" asked the captain.

"CARRY ME!"

"You've got to be joking!"

"CARRY ME!"

"But, Mr Bulk, you must weigh a tonne!"

"Two tonnes, actually! Now, come on, I just won the cup for you. Give this champ his victory lap. Come on!

PLEASE! CARRY ME!"

The boys shared a concerned look. The captain ordered them all to gather around their Sports teacher, and, on the count of three, to hoist him high into the air.

"ONE! TWO! THREE!"

Using all their might, they raised him up.

For a moment, they held his weight. But only for a moment. Their little arms gave way, and Bulk landed on top of them.

THUMP!

"HELP!"

"ARGH!"

"I AM BEING SQUASHED!"

Sadly, Mr Bulk never did get to do his victory lap. However, when all the boys in the TWADDLE team had got out of hospital, a special assembly was called. There, in front of the entire school, in a shiny new gold tracksuit with the letters **"G.O.A.T."** emblazoned on the back, Mr Bulk finally got his moment of glory. He held the **SCHOOLS' FOOTBALL CHAMPIONSHIPS** trophy above his head.

"YES! THE GREATEST OF ALL TIME!" he said as everyone cheered.

"HOORAY!"

To celebrate, he bit into a jumbo sausage sandwich.

MUNCH!

"BURP!"

PONG!

The burp was so meaty it actually formed a cloud that rained gravy.*

The events of this story are some years ago now, but Mr Bulk is still a teacher at TWADDLE SCHOOL . To this day, he bores the children senseless with wild boasts about his sporting achievements.

* It could happen. For all his genius, Sir Isaac Newton missed this one.

Of course, these stories are all twaddle. Except one.

The tale of the day he scored an incredible 397 goals.

That one is completely and utterly true.

The boys were right all along.

Mr Bulk really was

MRS SPLATT'S
Hall of Horrors

"EVIL" IS A STRONG WORD, but it is not strong
enough to describe Mrs Splatt. She was a dinner lady
who ruled with an iron fist. Literally. She only had one
real hand – the other was made of metal.

Legend had it that she'd stuck her hand in a tray of her

own gravy to retrieve a spoon, and the gravy was so toxic her hand had melted away.

FIZZLE! FAZZLE! FUZZLE!

Mrs Splatt's metal hand wasn't the only body part that had been added to her over the years.

Oh no.

One of her ears was rubber. It was shiny and much bigger than the other, and she couldn't hear out of it. The tale was she'd sliced her own ear off by mistake when she was chopping liver with an axe.

CHUNK!

Her left eye was made of glass. SLOP SCHOOL lore had it that it had popped out when she was beating a hunk of particularly tough meat into shape. As she saw it roll across the counter, she assumed it was a gobstopper, and swallowed it whole.

GULP!

Splatt also had a wooden leg. The story passed down through generations of pupils was that their dinner lady had fallen into a vat of her own piping-hot custard, and it had burned off.

SIZZLE! SAZZLE! SUZZLE!

Splatt also wore a frightful black wiry wig. Legend had it that she had burned all her hair and eyebrows off when she opened the oven door to take out a casserole she was cooking and it exploded. Underneath her wig, Splatt was as bald as an egg.

EGG

MRS SPLATT

She would whip off her wig when she needed to give one of her ancient pots or pans a jolly good scrub.

SCRUBBLE! SCRIBBLE! SCRABBLE!

As a result, it was full of burnt black bits and greasy brown bits.

Splatt had false teeth. The story was she'd lost them biting into one of her own rock cakes. Her rock cakes were infamous for being harder than concrete.

You might as well bite into a building. It would actually be tastier.

Splatt's false teeth rattled in her mouth.

RITTLE! ROTTLE! RUTTLE!

Sometimes they even flew out

when she shouted at someone.

"COME BACK 'ERE, YOU VERMIN…!"*

DOINK! "OUCH!"

Mrs Splatt had been the dinner lady at **SLOP SCHOOL** for longer than anyone could remember.

No one knew her age. She certainly looked ancient. Some put her in her eighties, others in her hundreds. A handful of children believed she may have been alive for thousands of years, like one of the undead, unable to die, destined to stalk the Earth for all eternity. That may well be true.

You might be interested to find out that the world's worst dinner ladies are all part of a secret society.

S.S.O.D.D.L.

That stands for

Secret Society of Dreadful Dinner Ladies

* She liked to call the children "vermin" even though diseased rodents were one of the main ingredients in her dinners.

S.S.O.D.D.L. meets up every Sunday night around midnight at a top-secret location* just before the school week begins. It is a chance for them to share disgusting recipes, swap cooking utensils (which double as instruments of torture) and elect a new supreme leader. Mrs Splatt has been the supreme leader of **S.S.O.D.D.L.** for fifty years. Despite the other dinner ladies being ferocious, no one ever dared challenge her. Would you?

* I am not able to reveal this location to you. If I did, I would have to go into hiding, as dinner ladies would track me down and force me to eat a tonne of boiled beetroot.

Mrs Splatt took great delight in serving up the most repulsive food she possibly could.

Most days it was her dreaded stew. She loved cooking stews, because she could bung anything she had in them. So today's stew might have all the leftovers of yesterday's stew in it. And yesterday's stew had all the leftovers of the stew from the day before. And so on, and so on. There was every chance you were eating last week's leftovers, or last month's, or last year's, or last decade's, or last century's.

Not just leftovers, though. Oh no. All kinds of things had been found **floating** around in Splatt's stinky stews:

A scouring pad

A pair of old man's underpants

A hedgehog

A flip-flop

A hearing aid

A used handkerchief (complete with snot stains)

A pair of laddered tights

A washing-up glove

A set of false
teeth

A mop and
bucket

A lint roller with
bits of hair still
stuck to it

A hamster's
wheel

A pair of
glasses

A walking
stick

A doll with its
head missing

A doll's
head

A lady's shoe (one of
a pair, presumably)

A shopping
trolley

A shuttlecock

A sock

A man
called Clive

"Hello, my
name is Clive."

There would be BIG TROUBLE for anyone at
SLOP SCHOOL who did not finish everything on their
plate. Including the teachers. Mrs Splatt would loom
over them, wielding her iron ladle in her iron fist, until
they had eaten every last morsel. If they didn't, she
would strike them hard on the knuckles…

...and shout at them:

"LICK THE PLATE CLEAN, VERMIN!"

Of course, if everyone licked their plate clean, that saved time for Mrs Splatt on washing up too. So that was a BOON.

Eating school dinners was compulsory for everyone at SLOP SCHOOL . Packed lunches were strictly forbidden. Splatt made sure of that. She and her army of dinner ladies did stop-and-searches on everyone as they passed through the school gates each morning. Pockets and bags were emptied. Any offending crisps, cakes or chocolate bars would be confiscated by the dinner ladies, and then eaten by them.

MUNCH! MUNCH! MUNCH!

One time, Splatt even ate a wooden pencil case. It was brown and she had to make absolutely sure it wasn't chocolate.

KERUNCH!

She actually quite enjoyed it.

"YUM!"

Although her false teeth did become stuck in it.

"MY TEETH!"

Mrs Splatt oversaw a reign of TERROR at SLOP SCHOOL . Every single kid there lived in mortal fear of her.

Except one.

Chewy.

The girl was so called because she was ALWAYS chewing bubblegum, and was an expert bubble blower. Chewy could blow bubbles that would reach the size of beach balls before they popped.

The morning our story starts, Chewy was waltzing through the school gates, chewing bubblegum as usual.

CHEW! CHEW! CHEW!

Of course, Mrs Splatt was waiting for her, her army of dinner ladies fanned out behind.

"Spit that gum out, you vermin!" ordered Splatt, her one good eye staring at the child.

"Why, Mrs Splott?" replied the girl. She loved getting the lady's name wrong on purpose.

"It's Splatt, not Splott. And can't you read?"

With her iron finger, the dinner lady pointed to a huge sign she'd attached to the school building that read:

FOD IS FORBODDEN ON SCHOOLE PRIMISES

Spelling wasn't her strong suit.

"Bubblegum isn't food," stated the girl.

"Yes it is," argued Splatt.

"No it isn't."

"Well then, what is it, Miss Clever Knickers?"

"It's bubblegum."

The hundreds of kids who'd been gathering in the playground to witness this had a good chortle.

"HA! HA! HA!"

"SILENCE!" ordered Splatt. She punched her iron fist into her other hand.

THWACK!

"Ouch!" she whimpered. "Now, listen to me, child. It's in your mouth and you are chewing it so it MUST be food."

"I am sorry to say you are wrong, Mrs Splutt—"

"SPLATT!"

"Whatever. The thing with bubblegum is that you spit it out after you have chewed it. Which is what we would all love to do with your disgusting school dinners."

"HA! HA! HA!" chortled the kids.

With that, the girl burst a huge bubblegum bubble in the dinner lady's face…

POP!

…before swanning off.

"HA! HA! HA!"

Splatt peeled the pink layer off her face. Before she could get her revenge, the bell rang for the first lesson of the day.

D R I N G !

She was boiling with anger. She had been made to look a fool. Now she was determined to break this "vermin", once and for all.

Splatt limped to the dining hall, or **HALL OF HORRORS** as the SLOP KIDS called it.

THUD! THUD! THUD! went her wooden leg.

Once in her kitchen, the dinner lady began hatching an EVIL PLAN.

"Today," she announced to her army of dinner ladies, "we will create the most repulsive, inedible, deadly dinner of all time!"

"I thought we did that every day," piped up the one with the glasses.

"We do, thank you, but today I want to teach that *vermin* a lesson she will never forget."

"Chewy!" exclaimed the one with the crooked nose.

"Yes. You guessed it! I want the food we serve up today to send that nasty little child running for the hills!"

A cheer went up in the kitchen.

"HURRAH!"

Immediately, the dinner ladies set to work. By noon, Splatt and her gang had created the most repulsive school-dinner menu of all time.

DRING!

The bell rang for lunchtime. Splatt whipped off her wig, gave the counter a quick mop, plonked the wig back on and took her place behind the trays of food, if they could be called that.

Her iron ladle was in her iron fist, her one good ear listening out for Chewy, and her one good eye looking out for her.

As soon as Chewy pushed the double doors open to the dining room…

CLUNK!

…the girl was shocked by the smell.

PONG!

The food always stank, but today the stink was enough to knock you out.

POOONNNGGG!

All the pupils and teachers of **SLOP SCHOOL** were choking and coughing, their eyes streaming.

"AHEM! AHEM! AHEM!"

"WATER! WATER!"

"CALL AN AMBULANCE!"

Pinching her nose with her fingers, Chewy nervously approached the food counter. Bubbling away was something that looked like a stew, even though it smelled like a campsite toilet.*

"We meet again, child," purred Splatt.

"Good afternoon, Mrs Splitt," chirped the girl.

"SPLATT!"

"That's what I said. Splutt. What kind of stew is this?"

"**STEW STEW!**" thundered Splatt, her false teeth shooting across the **HALL OF HORRORS.**

* If you have never been camping, then you will have to use your imagination. But, trust me, it was PONGTASTIC.**

** A real word you will find in your

WHIZZ!

They landed in some poor child's stinging-nettle soup.

DOINK!

SPLAT!

"YUCK!"

Fortunately, one of the dinner ladies, the one with the hairy chin, retrieved them for her glorious leader.

"I mean, what kind of meat is it?" asked the girl.

"Roadkill," replied Splatt, after replacing her false teeth. "It looked like a squirrel. It could be a fox. Or a big ginger rat. Hard to be sure. The lorry had squashed it flat. SPLUT!"

"Absolutely revolting!" was the girl's verdict.

"Thank you kindly, child," replied the dinner lady. That was high praise indeed.

"I am not eating that."

"No matter, no matter," purred the dinner lady, guiding the girl along the counter to something even more disgusting. "I also have this pie, straight from the oven."

The girl peered down at it.

"What kind of pie is it?" she asked.

"PIE PIE!" Once again, her false teeth made a dash for freedom.

WHIZZ!

They landed in a teacher's beetle blancmange.

SPLUT!

"EURGH!"

This time the dinner lady with the eyepatch retrieved Splatt's teeth for her.

"Have a slice!" ordered Splatt. "It's a surprise! My special **Pie Surprise!**"

Just then Chewy spotted that underneath the pastry top something had **moved!** It was **ALIVE!**

"What was that?" she demanded, seriously spooked.

"What was **what,** child?" replied the dinner lady, mock-innocently.

"Something moved under the pastry!"

Just then a claw appeared from underneath. Splatt whacked it with her ladle.

THWUCK!

"GRRRR!" Whatever was underneath that pastry top **growled.**

"I do pride myself on using only the freshest ingredients," announced Splatt.

"There's fresh and there's still alive! I am NEVER eating that!"

The dinner lady was growing tired of all this talking. She wanted the girl to do some eating, and fast.

"Well, there is still one more choice, child," she said, moving the girl further down the food counter. "And I have saved the best until last. Dumplings."

These "dumplings" were brown and steaming, and looked as if an animal had "laid" them that morning.

"They are not dumplings!" exclaimed the girl.

"Oh yes they are, child. I saw these dumplings being 'dumped' with my own eye! Hence the name!"

Splatt chuckled to herself. Behind her, the gang of dinner ladies chuckled too.

"HUH! HUH! HUH!"

The girl was adamant. "I am never, ever, ever, ever eating that!"

"Oh yes you are, child. That was your final choice. So, dumplings it is!"

Splatt went to ladle one of these brown steaming nightmares on to the girl's plate.

"NO!" shouted Chewy.

It was so loud that the **HALL OF HORRORS** descended into silence.

No one ever dared to say no to Mrs Splatt. All eyes turned to the dinner lady, who laughed her best evil laugh.

"HUH! HUH! HUH!"

She laughed so hard her false teeth shot out again, and landed in the stew.

SPLOTT!

It splashed the girl from head to toe.

"YUCK!" exclaimed Chewy.

Then she suddenly found herself feeling hotter than hot.

"OW! It's burning my skin!"

"Well, I do like my stews to be **SPICY,**" said the dinner lady. She reached her iron fist into the pot...

SIZZLE!

...and pulled out her false teeth, before pushing them back into her mouth.

"I AM NOT EATING ANY OF THIS MUCK!"

shouted the girl.

"You have to eat something, child," replied the dinner lady.

"WELL, I WILL NOT!" Chewy was defiant.

"Not even a pea?" suggested the dinner lady, mock-innocently.

"A pea?"

"Yes. An incy-wincy little pea. That couldn't do you any harm, now could it, child?"

The girl was feeling uneasy. It sounded like a trap.

"Just a pea?" asked Chewy.

"Just a pea."

"No sauce on it?"

"No sauce."

"Not spiced in any way?"

"No spice."

"Not stuffed with anything?"

"No stuffing."

"Then all right," announced Chewy.

"For my lunch today, I will have one pea!"

The dinner lady sported a **ghoulish** grin.

"One pea coming right up, child!"

Chewy looked around the troughs of food. There were mountains of the vegetables kids always hated – Brussels sprouts, beetroot, rhubarb, cabbage, broccoli – but no sign whatsoever of peas. Not one.

"Where exactly is this pea?" demanded the girl.

"I am just keeping it warm, child!" replied Splatt.

Then the dinner lady began making the most awful noises with her nose.

SNORT! SNURT! SNART!

"What on earth are you doing?" asked the girl.

"Just retrieving your pea!"

SNERT! SNIRT! SNORT!

With one final snort, a green pellet flew out of her nose and landed on the girl's plate with a D I N G !

The girl stared down at it.

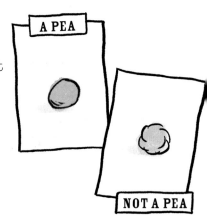

A PEA

NOT A PEA

"That's not a pea," she said, not unreasonably.

"What is it, then, child?" purred Splatt.

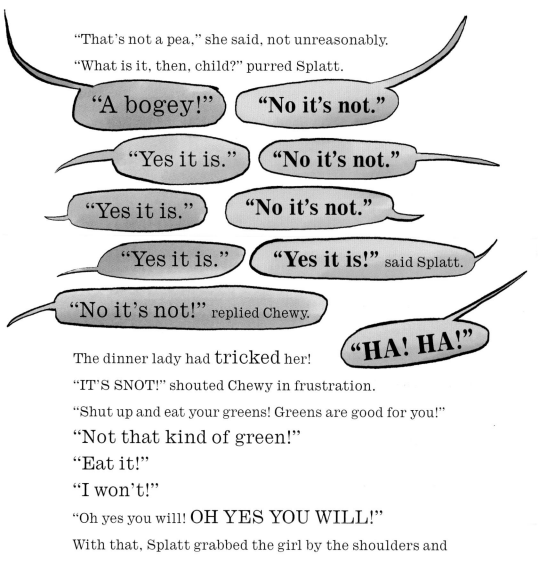

"A bogey!" **"No it's not."**

"Yes it is." **"No it's not."**

"Yes it is." **"No it's not."**

"Yes it is." **"Yes it is!"** said Splatt.

"No it's not!" replied Chewy.

"HA! HA!"

The dinner lady had tricked her!

"IT'S SNOT!" shouted Chewy in frustration.

"Shut up and eat your greens! Greens are good for you!"

"Not that kind of green!"

"Eat it!"

"I won't!"

"Oh yes you will! OH YES YOU WILL!"

With that, Splatt grabbed the girl by the shoulders and sat her down on the bench.

"EAT, VERMIN, EAT!" she ordered.

"NO!"

The dinner lady smashed her iron fist down

on the dining table…

THUD!

…throwing all the plates up into the air.

TRING!

CLATTER! CLUTTER! CLOTTER!

The children sitting at the table were covered in stew and pie and dumplings.

"URGH!" they cried. It was disgusting being coated in the stuff, although it was preferable to eating it.

"EAT IT! OR I PROMISE THERE WILL BE HELL TO PAY!" shouted Splatt. Once again, her false teeth went flying…

WHIZZ!

…hitting a boy on the head…

DOINK!

He landed face down in his stew.

SPLUT!

"I SAID, 'NO'!" shouted the girl.

Splatt was so frustrated she shouted, "VERMIN!" and thumped the wall with her iron fist.

DUNK!

A cloud of dust exploded across the room.

BOOSH!

Everyone began coughing and spluttering.

"AHEM! AHEM! AHEM!"

Splatt strained to remove her fist

from the wall but she couldn't.

"EURGH! EURGH! EURGH!"

Her fist was stuck there.

She yanked and yanked and yanked,

but it just wouldn't budge.

"LOOK WHAT YOU HAVE DONE TO MY BLASTED HAND, CHILD!" she growled.

The dinner lady pushed her foot up against the wall to act as a lever. She tugged and tugged and tugged, before...

PLUP!

...her arm popped clean out of her metal hand.

"NO!" shouted the dinner lady.

Without her iron fist, Splatt felt powerless. Not thinking, she unscrewed her wooden leg so that she could instil terror.

ROLL! ROLL! ROLL!

She bashed the dining table with it. *BOOSH!*

"THAT WILL BE YOU NEXT, VERMIN!"

If she had thought first, Splatt would have realised that, unlike the flamingo, she was unable to stand on one leg. A look of horror flashed across her face as she realised she had lost her balance.

"NOOO!" *PLONK!*

Before she knew it, Splatt was lying face down on the greasy floor of the dining room.

"OUCH!"

To make matters worse, her glass eye popped out of its socket, and rolled across the floor. *RRROOOLLLLLLL!*

As she scrambled to her knee, her rubber ear dropped off.

THWUCK!

She picked it up, and scared the children with it by sticking it right in their faces. "EURGH!" "NOOO!" "HELP!"

"DON'T THINK I CAN'T HEAR YOU, CHILDREN!" she roared. "NOW, VERMIN, EAT THAT PEA!"

"NO," shouted Chewy.

In frustration, Splatt yanked off her wig and threw it at the girl.

WHOOOOOOOOOOOSH!

Chewy ducked, and it landed in the stew of the elderly History teacher, Mr Antiquate.

SPLOSH!

"Excuse me, madam," he began, "I think there's a hair in my stew."

Still, the old man carried on eating. He actually enjoyed Mrs Splatt's food, but he was the only one.

The dinner lady was now half the woman she had been, having lost a leg, a hand, her wig, her left eye and her left ear. Still she was coming straight for Chewy.

"YOU WILL EAT MY SNOT, YOU VERMIN, IF IT'S THE LAST THING YOU DO!"

"Oh no I won't!"

As quick as a flash, the girl reached into her blazer pocket and pulled out a jumbo pack of bubblegum.

The brand was

Once unwrapped, she stuffed the entire pack of

DOUBLE BUBBLE into her mouth and began chewing

like a maniac.

"MMM! MMM! MMM!"

Then, as soon as she could, Chewy began blowing a

bubble.

SHH! SHHH! SHHHH!

"NO GUM IN THE DINING ROOM,

VERMIN!" roared Splatt from the dining-room floor.

Still Chewy blew and blew and blew

and blew.

SHHH!

First the bubble was the size of a ping-pong ball.

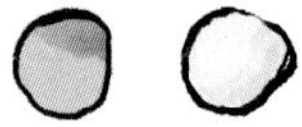

SHHHH!

Then it was the size of a watermelon.

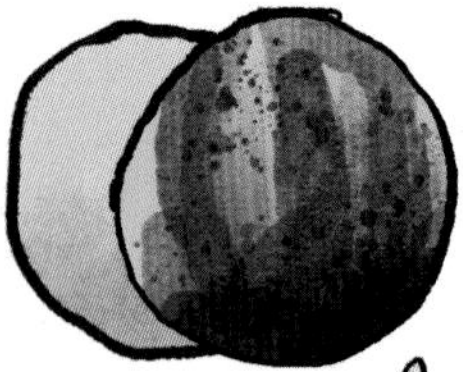

"SPIT THAT OUT AT ONCE!"

SHHHHH!

Next it was the size of a globe.

SHHHHHH!

Eventually it was the size of a hot-air balloon.

"I AM GOING TO POP YOUR BUBBLE FOR THE LAST TIME!"

Splatt lifted up her finger to the bubble and tried to stab it with her dirty great nail.

JAB! JAB! JAB!

But, instead of popping, the bubble enveloped Mrs Splatt.

In no time at all, the dinner lady was trapped inside it.

"LET ME OUT, YOU VERMIN! LET ME OUT!" she cried, slamming her hand against the wall of pink bubblegum that imprisoned her.

THWACK!

THWACK!

THWACK!

"I NEED ALL YOUR HELP, KIDS!" called out Chewy. **"EVERY SINGLE ONE OF YOU!"**

The children in the dining room all leaped to their feet.

"Hold the doors open!" ordered the girl.

The nearest two children to the dining-room double doors did just that.

"The rest of you, gather around me, and blow!"

"Blow?" asked the littlest boy.

"Trust me! This will only work if we all do it! THREE! TWO! ONE! BLOW!"

All at once, the children did what she said. They pursed their lips and blew as hard as they could.

WHOOOOOOOO

Together the kids of SLOP SCHOOL created a gust of wind that was so powerful it blew the giant bubblegum bubble, with Splatt trapped inside it, out of the **HALL OF HORRORS.** The dinner ladies all looked on in wonder as their glorious leader floated past them.

"NOOOO!"

cried Splatt, bashing
against the wall of
bubblegum. She tried
to spit her false teeth
out to make a hole.

— "SPLATT!" —

OOOSH!

But the teeth bounced off the pink wall and
whacked her right on the nose. BOINK!

"OUCH!" she screamed as she sailed through the
doors, and out into the playground.

"KIDS! FOLLOW HER! AND KEEP
BLOWING!" ordered Chewy.

wHOOOOOOOOOOOOSH!

Soon, the kids had the bubble floating high in the air.
Before you knew it, the evil Mrs Splatt was nothing
more than a tiny pink dot in the sky.

"GOODBYE!" called out Chewy. "Us vermin are so going to miss you!"

All the kids laughed heartily.

"HA! HA! HA!"

"Right! Now let's order some pizza!" shouted the girl.

"YES!" they all cheered.

MR PHOBE'S
FEAR

NOT ALL OF THE world's worst teachers are **VILLAINS.**
Some are just very, very, very bad teachers.

   This is the story of a very, very, very, very, very
bad teacher. A teacher so bad, in fact, that he never, ever
taught.

MR PHOBE'S FEAR

A teacher who doesn't teach? What nonsense is this?
Please let me explain. Mr Phobe was a HEAD teacher.
Mr Phobe was in many ways a model teacher with
his:

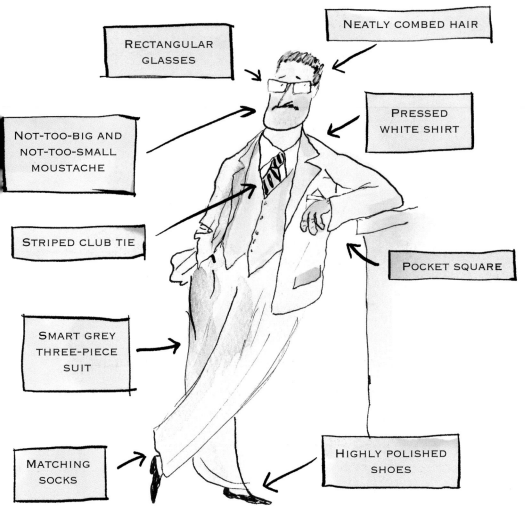

NEATLY COMBED HAIR

RECTANGULAR GLASSES

PRESSED WHITE SHIRT

NOT-TOO-BIG AND NOT-TOO-SMALL MOUSTACHE

STRIPED CLUB TIE

POCKET SQUARE

SMART GREY THREE-PIECE SUIT

MATCHING SOCKS

HIGHLY POLISHED SHOES

However, Mr Phobe had a **fear**. A frightful **fear** that made his...

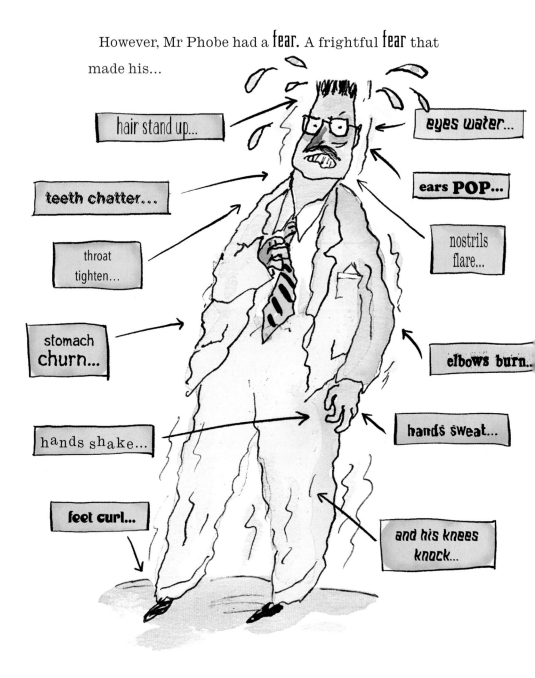

hair stand up...

eyes water...

teeth chatter...

ears **POP**...

throat tighten...

nostrils flare...

stomach churn...

elbows burn..

hands shake...

hands sweat...

feet curl...

and his knees knock...

It was a **fear** so huge that when Mr Phobe was confronted with it he would *SCREAM* the school down.

"ARGH!"

Then he would run and hide. The headmaster had hiding places all over the school:

Under his desk

In the cleaning cupboard

Behind some books on a shelf in the library

Up
a climbing
frame

In the
trophy
cabinet

Inside a tuba

Inside the lost-property
basket under some
smelly socks

PONG!

Under the dinner
lady's apron

Under a pile of leaves

Inside a drawer

Mr Phobe would do absolutely **anything** to get away
from what **terrified** him the most.

So **what** was he so scared of?

I will tell you...

Children!

That's right – the headmaster had a terrible **fear** of children.

Children just like **you**.

But how could this be? A teacher scared of children? Surely it is the other way round! Children should be terrified of **teachers!**

Not in this case.

Please let me take you back in time, fifty years ago, to the day when this story begins.

It was Mr Phobe's very **first day** as a teacher.

He was just twenty-one, fresh out of teacher-training college, and ready to take on the world. Mr Phobe started as a supply teacher, which is stepping in at a school when one of their teachers is off sick.*

Little did he know that on his very first day of work the young Mr Phobe was being sent to the school with the **worst-behaved** children in the **entire** world –

HELL'S BELLS SCHOOL
FOR HORRIBLE BOYS

* Or, more likely, had been driven bananas by the pupils!

At this school, if it could be called a school (it was more like a boys' prison, one where the prisoners were in charge), the pupils ran **riot.** There were food fights every lunchtime in the dining hall...

SPLAT!

running battles in the Sports hall...

BISH! BASH! **BOSH!**

explosions in the Science block...

KABOOM!

football games in the classrooms...

SMASH!

paint splashed all over the Art room... **SPLOSH!**

clumps of wet bog roll stuck to the ceiling of the toilet...

SPLUT!

heavy metal blaring from the music room...

DUM! DUM! DUM!

skateboard races in the corridors...

W H I Z Z !

a crocodile that had been

"borrowed" from the local zoo,

lurking in the pond...

SNAP!

food trays used as sledges

on the stairs...

CLUNK!

CLUNK!

CLUNK!

and dinner ladies tied

to goal posts...

"HELP!"

Needless to say, teachers didn't last long at **HELL'S BELLS.** The average length of time any of them stayed at the school was two days. Two days were enough to have any teacher running for the hills!

"THE HORROR! THE HORROR!" they would cry as they fled.

As well they might.

The young Mr Phobe knew nothing about the terrible reputation of **HELL'S BELLS.** All he knew when he woke up in the morning and received the telephone call was that he was replacing a Mr Mildmanner. He was a History teacher who had mysteriously "disappeared" on a rare **HELL'S BELLS** school visit to a medieval castle.*

That fateful morning, Mr Phobe marched confidently into the History classroom at **HELL'S BELLS.** His shiny new briefcase was swinging in his hand, his rolled-up umbrella was tucked under his arm and he was humming a happy tune to himself.

"DA-DE-DA-DE-DA..."

* Mr Mildmanner was found ten years later, in rags with a long white beard, locked in the castle dungeon. He had survived by eating cockroaches.

This was what all those years of hard work at college had been leading up to. Mr Phobe was now a fully qualified teacher! He was ready to change lives, shape young minds, be a role model to **generations of children.** The teacher took a deep breath, smiled broadly and flung open the classroom door.

The poor man hadn't even uttered a word when a bucket of *custard* fell from the top of the door.

CLATTER!

SPLAT!

Now not only was he covered from head to toe in thick yellow **goo** but he had thirty terrors pointing and laughing at him.

"HA! HA! HA!"

The **HELL'S BELLS** boys were startling to behold. It was as if they'd been living wild in a jungle all their lives, having been looked after by a troop of apes.

Hair was long and unwashed...

Long trousers had been torn into shorts...

Knees were scabbed...

Shoes were scuffed...

Shirts were grubby and ripped...

Ties were tied round heads...

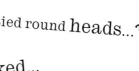

Glasses were cracked...

Blazers had been abandoned...

Eyes were blackened...

Teeth were missing...

Poor Mr Phobe felt like bursting into floods of tears at being coated in custard, but decided it was best NOT to react. That was exactly what these **MONSTERS** wanted. To see their latest victim cry. Or shout. Or run straight back out of the classroom.

So Mr Phobe decided to completely ignore what had just happened.

He marched over to the chalkboard...

SQUELCH! SQUELCH! SQUELCH!

...and turned to face the class.

"G-g-good m-m-morning," he began.

NOOOO! he thought.

His voice had come out all high and wavering because he was n-n-n-n-n-n-n-nervous.

Just then a toilet plunger zoomed through the air...

W H I Z Z !

...and hit him – **BANG!** – on the forehead.

P L U N K !

The boys rocked with laughter. "HA! HA! HA!"

Again, Mr Phobe chose to ignore this. The new teacher carried on as if it were perfectly normal for him to be

about to begin a lesson
coated in custard with a
toilet plunger stuck to his
forehead. Calmly, he put down
his briefcase and picked up a
piece of chalk.

Noticing the blackboard was awash with the rudest words known to man...

...he quickly rubbed them off. **RUB! RUB! RUB!**

Next, the teacher began chalking his name on the board.

Because he was so n-n-n-n-n-n-n-n-n-n-nervous, his hand was wobbling.

WIBBLE! WOBBLE! WABBLE!

The chalk was tapping against the board.

TAP! TIP! TOP!

It was impossible to keep his hand steady.

So, instead of writing "Mr Phobe", he'd actually scrawled something else entirely: "Mrs Phoooooo".

As soon as Mr Phobe turned round and revealed what he'd scrawled on the board, the brutes hooted with laughter again.

"HA! HA! HA!"

This was immediately followed by calls of,
"Good morning, **Mrs Phoooooo**! HA! HA! HA!"

Being children, they found this hilarious, because
it sounded a lot like "poo", and for some reason poo is
always, always, always funny.*

Little did Mr Phobe know that his ordeal at the hands
of the **HELL'S BELLS** boys was only just beginning.

"Now t-t-t-today I am t-t-t-t-taking over f-f-f-from Mr
M-M-M-M-M..." The teacher's n-n-n-n-n-n-n-n-
n-n-n-n-n-n-n-n-n-erves were getting the better of him.
The poor man couldn't get his words out.

"**Mr Meatballs?**" suggested Mungo, the gobbiest one
at the back of the class.

"HA! HA! HA!"

"N-n-n-o, n-n-n-n-o, Mr..."

"**Mr Monkey-Doo-Doo?**"
asked Dooby, the next gobbiest one near the
back of the class.

"HA! HA! HA!"

"N-N-N-N-NO! N-N-N-N-N-NO!
Mr..."

"**Mr Mardy-Bum?**" said another.

* Thank goodness, as I have made a career out of
poo jokes.

"HA! HA! HA!"

"N-N-N-N-N-N-N-N-N-N-N-N-NO!"

"Mr Mashed-Potato?"

"HA! HA! HA!"

"N-N-N-N-N-N-N-N-N-N-N-N-N-N-N-N-N-N-NO!"

"Mr Minger?"

"HA! HA! HA!"

Poor Mr Phobe couldn't take any more.

"N-N-N-N-N-N-N-N-N-N-N-N-N-N-N-N-N-N-N-N-N-N-N-N-N-N-N-N-N-N-N-N-N-N-N-N-N-N-N-N-N-N-N-N-NOO OOOOOOOOOOOOOOOOOOOOOOO OOOOOOOOOOOOOOOOOOOOO OOOOOOOOO!" he screamed.

It was so **LOUD** the walls wobbled.

Finally, SILENCE descended upon the classroom for what was the first time in years.

It was not to last.

For a glorious golden moment, Mr Phobe believed he'd finally won their respect.

How wrong he was.

 exclaimed the entire class.

"Now come on, settle down!" he ordered.

On Mungo's prompt, the **horrors** all repeated exactly what their new supply teacher had just said.

"NOW COME ON, SETTLE DOWN!"

came a chorus of replies.

The teacher shook his head, and rolled his eyes.

"This is just stupid."

"THIS IS JUST STUPID!"

"Stop repeating everything I say!"

"STOP REPEATING EVERYTHING I SAY!"

"RIGHT! THAT'S IT! I'VE HAD ENOUGH!"

"RIGHT! THAT'S IT! I'VE HAD ENOUGH!"

Mr Phobe couldn't take any more. He closed his eyes.

As soon as he did, he felt a tomato **explode** across his face. W H O O S H !

"HA! HA! HA!"

"No one tell him it was me who threw it!" hissed a voice.

"Right you are, Dooby," came a reply.

"DOH!"

Mr Phobe opened his eyes, and began to speak, slowly and softly.

"I want to tell you kids something. I know it's not cool or trendy, but I became a teacher because I want to make the world a better place. You kids are the future. If I can make just one of you be the best you can be, then I can give myself a big pat on the back."

His voice was growing louder as his speech gathered momentum.

"So, come on, kids, who is with me? Who wants to be the bestest best they can be? Who wants to learn about... THE INDUSTRIAL REVOLUTION?"

The boys all leaped to their feet and burst into applause. In unison, they shouted,

"YES!"

A proud tear welled in the teacher's eye.

HE HAD TURNED THESE **BEASTS** AROUND!

"Sir?" began Mungo. "I think I speak for all of us here by saying thank you from the bottom of our hearts and the hearts of our bottoms for inspiring us."

"It is my great pleasure," croaked Mr Phobe. "Let's begin the History lesson! Let's find out about the transference to new manufacturing processes from *1760* to *1840!* Let's learn! Let's grow! KIDS, LET'S REACH FOR THE STARS!"

"LET'S DO IT!" they all replied.

"We can't wait to learn about the increasing use of steam and water power, the development of machine tools and the rise of the mechanised factory system!" exclaimed Mungo.

"YES!" replied Mr Phobe, punching the air.

"Just take a seat, sir, and then we can begin!"

Mungo's grin oozed around the classroom until it had spread across the faces of all the boys.

"KIDS! LET'S DO THIS!" proclaimed Mr Phobe, slamming himself down on to his chair.

DOOF!

Instantly, he wished he hadn't. The **horrors** had covered the seat with hundreds of drawing pins!*

NICK! NICK! NICK! NICK! NICK! NICK!

"OOOWWWWEEE!" screamed Mr Phobe. As well you might if you had hundreds of drawing pins stuck to your bottom.

"HA! HA! HA!"

In desperation, the teacher began hopping around the classroom.

HIP! HOP! HIPPIE! HIPPITY! HOP!

That didn't work.

Neither did jumping.

DOING! DOING! DOING!

* Do not try this at home, at school or anywhere. No one likes a perforated bottom.

Or even cartwheeling.

W H O O S H !

All this achieved was to make the

brutes howl even louder with laughter.

"HA! HA! HA!"

"IT FEELS LIKE MY BOTTY

IS ON FIRE!" cried Mr Phobe as

he charged towards the classroom door. His

foot became stuck in an old tin bucket, but he carried on

regardless.

CLUTTER! CLATTER! CLOTTER!

"WATER! WATER!" he cried.

As he hurried along the corridor,
all the terrors followed. Clutching
his bottom, Mr Phobe found the
nearest bathroom. He charged
inside and found the closest
cubicle. With no time to lose,
the teacher lifted the seat and
plunged his bottom into
the bowl.

"AAAHHH!" he sighed as the cold water lapped around his burning buttocks. SIZZLE!

To anyone who might be passing, Mr Phobe was quite a sight. The teacher was covered from head to toe in custard, with a tomato splattered across his face, a toilet plunger stuck to his forehead and his bottom wedged down the loo.

In no time, the swine caught up with him.

One by one, their nasty little faces appeared round the door.

"HA! HA! HA!" they all laughed.

Mungo shook his head, and took charge.

"QUIET, BOYS!" he ordered, and they were quiet.

"Wonderful speech, Mrs Phoooo."

"Thank you," he muttered, trying to make the best of this most undignified position he had found himself in.

"I am so, SO sorry this happened, Mrs Phoooo," Mungo continued, clutching his chest to appear even more sincere than he sounded.

"That's quite all right, um...?" began the teacher.

"Mungo."

"Mungo. I suppose accidents do happen," he continued, trying to put a brave face on things.

"But on your very first day at **HELL'S BELLS?** Tut, tut, tut. What rotten luck. How is your bottom now, **Mrs Phooo?"**

"Still piping hot, I'm afraid. And it's Mr Phobe."

"That's what I said, **Mrs Phooo!"** replied Mungo, smirking. "Maybe you need some more cold water."

"Oh no, I don't think—"

"Let me help, sir!"

With that, the boy reached across the teacher and pressed the flush.

PLONK! SPLOSH!

"NOOO!" cried Mr Phobe.

The poor man didn't stand a chance. With his bottom so far down the bowl, the suction from below dragged him downwards.

W H O O M P H !

"HELP!" he yelled.

But it was too late.

Mr Phobe was flushed down the toilet.
KERSPLUNK!

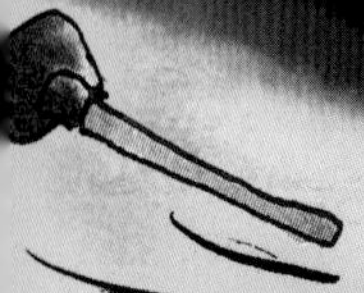

S W I R L !

GURGLE! GURGLE! GURGLE!

"Farewell, Mrs Phooo!"

called out the monsters.
"HA! HA! HA!"

Dooby, grinning devilishly, whipped a stopwatch out of his pocket. "Mr Phobe lasted a mere four minutes and seventeen seconds at the school!"

"That's a new record!" exclaimed Mungo. "Well done, us!"

"HOORAY!"

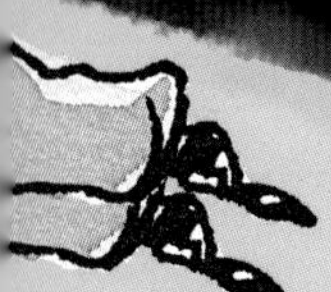

Meanwhile, Mr Phobe was being sucked through a never-ending maze of pipes and tubes.

SQUISH!

SQUASH!

SQUESH!

Finally, with the toilet plunger still stuck to his head, he found himself coming up for air.

"GASP!"

It was then that Mr Phobe realised the impossible.

Things had taken a turn for the worse.

The much worse.

He was in a **sewage** plant.

The teacher was swimming in a steaming pool of **poo**!

PONGY-WONGY-WOO!

"NOOOOOOOOOOOOOOOOOOOOOOOoooooooo ooooooooooooooooooooooooooo!" he cried.

From that fateful day forward, Mr Phobe did everything he possibly could to avoid children at all costs. The safest way, he thought, was to become a headmaster. Then he could hide in his office all day, shuffling his paperwork and NOT meeting any little **horrors.**

Little **horrors** just like you.

So, if one day you see Mr Phobe locking himself in a locker, or diving into a hedge, or furiously burying himself in the football pitch, please remember something.

It's not his fault he is t-t-t-t-t-t-t-t-t-t-t-t-t-t- t-t-t-t-t-t-t-terrified of children.

After all, Mr Phobe had once been flushed down a toilet.

KERSPLOSH!